Dear Reader,

I can hardly believe that it is almost twenty years since I wrote my first Harlequin book. The thrill of having that book accepted and then seeing it on the bookshelves—being picked up and chosen by readers—is one I shall never forget.

Twenty years seems a long time. So much has happened during those years; so much has changed and yet so much remains the same. The changes that we have all seen within society are, I believe, reflected in the books we, as Harlequin authors, write. They mirror the changes that take place around us in our own and our readers' lives. Our heroines have changed, matured, grown up, as indeed I have done myself. I cannot tell you how much pleasure it gives me to be able to write of mature—as well as young— women finding love. And, of course, love is something that has not changed. Love is still love and always will be, because love is, after all, an intrinsic, vital component of human happiness.

As I read through these books that are being reissued in this Collector's Edition, they bring back for me many happy memories of the times when I wrote them, and I hope that my readers, too, will enjoy the same nostalgia and pleasure.

I wish you all very many hours of happy reading and lives blessed with love.

Penny Jordan

Back by Popular Demand

Penny Jordan is one of the world's best loved as well as bestselling authors, and she was first published by Harlequin in 1981. The novel that launched her career was *Falcon's Prey*, and since then she has gone on to write more than one hundred books. In this special collection, Harlequin is proud to bring back a selection of these highly sought after novels. With beautiful cover art created by artist Erica Just, this is a Collector's Edition to cherish.

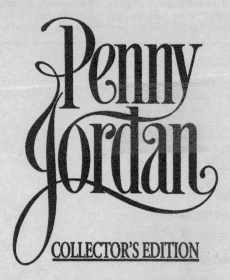

Penny Jordan

COLLECTOR'S EDITION

Desire Never Changes

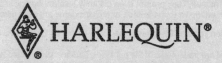

HARLEQUIN®

TORONTO • NEW YORK • LONDON
AMSTERDAM • PARIS • SYDNEY • HAMBURG
STOCKHOLM • ATHENS • TOKYO • MILAN • MADRID
PRAGUE • WARSAW • BUDAPEST • AUCKLAND

ISBN 0-373-63069-7

DESIRE NEVER CHANGES

First North American Publication 1987.

Copyright © 1986 by Penny Jordan.

This edition published by arrangement with Harlequin Books S.A.

® and TM are trademarks of the publisher. Trademarks indicated with
® are registered in the United States Patent and Trademark Office, the
Canadian Trade Marks Office and in other countries.

Visit us at www.romance.net

Printed in U.S.A.

ERICA JUST
cover illustrator for the
Penny Jordan Collector's Edition

Erica Just is an artist and illustrator working in various media, including watercolor, pen and ink, and textiles. Her studio is in Nottingham, England.

Her work is inspired by the natural forms, architecture and vibrant colors that she has experienced on her travels, most especially in Africa and India.

Erica has exhibited her work extensively in Great Britain and Europe and has works in private and public collections. As an illustrator she works for a number of companies and also lectures on textile design throughout the country.

CHAPTER ONE

'SOMER, you're sure you'll be all right?'

'Daddy, of course I will.' Soft dimples showed briefly in the delicate, pale skin Somer had often been told was a true Celtic heritage, along with her fine black hair and eyes which changed from stormy grey to glowing amethyst, depending on her mood. Today they glowed an excited violet, her impatience with her father's concern hastily suppressed as she tried to console him. It was barely three months since she had left school and come home to Scotland and her father was still very obviously bemused by her swift transition from girl-child to woman.

He had been concerned when she first told him that she and Andrew wanted to get engaged, pointing out that she was only eighteen and knew nothing of life. Much as her own mother must have been at the same age, Somer had countered resolutely, and yet *she* had been a mother at nineteen. Her father's face had clouded when she mentioned her mother. It was ten years since she had died, and Somer's baby brother with her, but Sir Duncan MacDonald had never married again. He had been just another poor Highland laird when he had married Catriona Sefton, but now he was a very wealthy man; a large shareholder in the North Sea's privately owned Sefton oilfield, named after his wife, and although he didn't communicate them to Somer, he had all a wealthy father's fears for his only daughter. He sighed, looking at her, her small, heart-shaped face glowing with excitement and anticipation. Six months ago at Christmas he had been away in the Middle East on business and she had not been able to come home from school. Instead she had accepted an invitation to stay with a school-friend and her family on Jersey and it was there that she had met Andrew Hollister—had met him and fallen wildly in love with him.

Duncan MacDonald had not yet met his prospective son-in-law. Andrew was in hotel management and worked at an hotel in Jersey. He and Somer had corresponded when she went back to school and Somer had spent Easter with him, returning with the small solitaire engagement ring which she had worn ever since.

She had wanted to be married straight away but her father had prevailed upon her to wait at least until she was nineteen. Because she loved him she had agreed, and now as she waited to board her plane Somer glanced worriedly at him. Although he had not said so, she sensed that her father did not entirely approve of her engagement. She knew that he thought eighteen was too young to commit herself to marriage, but *she* knew how she felt about Andrew; knew that their love would last for ever. Her father had forgotten what it was like to be eighteen and so deeply in love that every second apart was unbearable agony. She glanced down at her engagement ring, watching the prisms of light thrown off by the small diamond, remembering how tenderly Andrew had kissed her finger as he slid it into place.

Boarding school had kept her rather more innocent than most girls her age; the only boys she had met prior to Andrew had been the brothers of school-friends, or boys from a neighbouring boys' school. Andrew at twenty-four to her eighteen had dazzled her with his easy charm; his warm smile and the careless touch of his fingers against her skin, promising undreamed of delights and yet experienced enough to know that she wasn't yet quite ready for the intimacies of lovers. They would wait until they were married, he had whispered at Easter, when his passionate kisses had made her take fright, and her heart had swelled with love and gratitude for his understanding.

But now her father was insisting that they wait until she was nineteen—nine long months away and during that time Andrew could be posted anywhere by his company. The first time they met he had told her of his hopes and plans for the future, unburdening himself to her in a way which had made her feel very grown up. Andrew wanted to own his own hotel, a luxurious Eden catering for the wealthy, preferably in the Caribbean, but he had a long way to go before he reached that goal, he had told Somer ruefully. He had been acting Assistant Manager at the Group's Jersey hotel for nearly eighteen months and was hoping for an early promotion.

'Just think, we could start our married life in Barbados,' he had told Somer at Easter, and although she had been thrilled to hear him talk of their life together, there had been pain as well in the knowledge that a posting to Barbados would take her far away from the father she was only just beginning to know. On her return from school her father had suggested that she might care to act as his hostess. His position as head of Sefton Oil involved a great deal of business entertaining, of visiting other oil-producing countries and of entertaining overseas visitors in return, and after her first month at home which had been filled with apprehension and fear Somer had discovered that she actually enjoyed her new role and that she seemed to have a talent for it. Her father's Aberdeen home was large and gracious and he employed an excellent cook-cum-housekeeper, Mrs McLeod, who had warmly welcomed Somer's assistance.

'There's my flight now,' Somer told her father, 'I'd better go.' She reached up, kissing his cheek. 'Daddy, please stop worrying. I love Andrew and he loves me. Everything's going to be fine.'

The smile he gave her was slightly strained, and he wondered what his daughter would say if she knew of the investigations he had had carried out on the man she loved. They had shown nothing to his detriment. He had no money apart from his salary, but there had been a time when Duncan MacDonald himself had been in that position and he was not the man to hold lack of wealth against another. He had enough money to support half a dozen sons-in-law. He moved closer to the barrier, intent on catching a final glimpse of Somer. Her heritage was all Celtic and there had been times after his wife's death when he had worried about his delicately strung daughter, so quick to feel pain, both her own and that of others, but there was always that bedrock of MacDonald pride for her to fall back on; that grim resoluteness that acted as a counterweight to her Celtic mysticism. This was her heritage, and he could no more stop her from receiving it than he could hold back the tides.

Safely on board the plane taking her to Andrew, Somer had no inkling of the sombreness of her father's thoughts. Named after Somerled, the great warrior Lord of the Isles, her mind was not on the past but firmly riveted on her golden future. Of course Andrew would be as disappointed as she was that they could not be married sooner. He had urged her to try to persuade her father to change his mind, but she knew he would understand that she felt that she could not do so. That was one of the things she most liked about Andrew. He was so understanding, so caring of other people's views; he had even chided her gently when she had come close to losing her temper when her father had urged her not to marry straight away. 'It's only natural that he should want to keep you a little longer,' he had told her with that whimsical smile of his that made her heart flutter so. 'And I can afford to be generous. After all I'll have you for the rest of our lives.'

Dear, darling Andrew. She closed her eyes and lay back in her seat, slowly visualising him, her body trembling in anticipation of their reunion. She loved everything about him from the way his fair hair curled round his head to the hard compactness of his muscular body. It was true that he wasn't quite as tall as her father. Duncan Mac-Donald was well over six foot while Andrew stopped just short of five foot ten, but since she herself was barely five four, it hardly mattered. Elfin was the way he described her, and a shiver of apprehension suddenly ran through her. She wasn't particularly beautiful, not blonde or curvaceous; she lacked the self-possession of many of the other women Andrew knew. But it was her he loved, she reminded herself. As though to reassure herself that it wasn't all a dream she glanced down at her ring, and then extracted a small mirror from her bag, quickly checking her make-up. She wondered if Andrew would notice and approve of the new way she was doing her eyes. Soft, muted shadows enhanced their violet depths, a discreet rimming of kohl adding to their air of mystery. Her skin was without blemish, flawless and very fair. Too fair, she often thought, certainly too fair to expose unwarily to the sun. She thought rebelliously of the tanned holidaymakers frequenting the hotel at Easter, and then reminded herself that she was the one Andrew wanted; that it was her long night-black hair that he preferred; her slender body and pale skin.

'The trouble with you is that you just don't make enough of yourself.' That had been the criticism of Somer's greatest friend at school, the same outward-going, pretty brunette who had introduced her to Andrew. She had gained in self-confidence since meeting Andrew, but she knew she still had a long way to go before she came anywhere near to achieving the same smooth sophisticated self-confidence possessed by say, Judith Barnes, the senior receptionist at Andrew's hotel.

Judith was tall and blonde, with a heavy mane of hair that cascaded down on to her shoulders. Her face was always flawlessly made up, her clothes discreetly elegant. She had the sort of figure that men always gave a second glance, and Somer had sensed right from the start that Judith despised her, although she had no idea why. When she had tried tentatively to broach the subject with Andrew he had simply shrugged and laughed. 'Judith's a woman, little baby,' he had teased her. 'The sort of woman who's only really interested in men.'

'A man-eater.' That was how her friend Claire had described the receptionist, and yet Somer had sensed a very real antipathy towards her personally, in the older girl's manner, despite the politeness with which it was cloaked.

The flight to Jersey was only a short one, and it seemed to Somer that no sooner had she stepped on to the plane than she was stepping off into the bright July sunshine. Andrew had promised to meet her, but there was no sign of him by the time she had collected her luggage. She was just debating whether she ought to hire a taxi when a small white sports car came racing towards her, stopping with an impatient screech of tires only yards away.

When Judith Barnes stepped out, glamorous as always in a pair of dazzling white bermuda shorts and brief top in the same colour that clung to her curves and showed

off her deep tan, Somer felt her heart plummet downwards.
There would be no doubt that Judith had come to meet her
and that she was impatient, it showed in every line of her
elegant figure as she strode to where Somer was standing.

'Look, there's no hired help around here,' she announced curtly as she indicated the open boot of her car.
'The only way those cases are going to get back to the
hotel is if you pick them up. I've done my bit coming to
collect you and that's only because Drew asked me to.
What on earth have you brought with you?' she added with
arrogant amusement staring at the two large cases by Somer's side. 'A whole new wardrobe to bedazzle Drew?'
She laughed mockingly. 'Hasn't anyone ever told you that
all you need is what nature gave you? Although I suppose
in your case, she was a bit ungenerous.'

Cold blue eyes flicked from Somer's neatly suit-clad
figure to her own shapely body, and Somer felt a familiar
clenching of muscles inside her which she dimly recognised as intense anger. Firmly dismissing it, she picked up
one of her cases and carried it to the car, heaving it into
the boot before returning for the other.

The drive to the hotel was a tense one. In addition to
her disappointment that Andrew wasn't able to collect her,
Somer had to contend with her growing dislike of Judith.
The road they took was narrow, as indeed were most of
the island roads, and not built for high speeds, but despite
this Judith insisted on driving well in excess of the limit,
and on several occasions Somer was forced to clutch on
to the side of the car as they screeched dangerously round
a bend.

'Scared?' Judith mocked as she took the turn that led
down to the Hermitage Hotel and its private beach. 'Poor
little scaredy-girl, how on earth are you going to keep

Drew, if you're scared of a little bit of speed? Little girls should stick to their own league,' she added tauntingly.

Somer said nothing, unable to trust herself to speak without betraying the temper she could feel raging through her. 'Never say anything in the first heat of anger,' her father had once warned her. 'It's a common MacDonald failing, and one our clan has had to pay dearly for in the past. Always count to ten, always think about the repercussions of what you're going to say.'

It had been good advice; she recognised that and so now she averted her face and concentrated on Andrew's image, denying Judith the satisfaction of knowing that her barbs had hurt.

The hotel forecourt was full of cars, a sign that business was good, Somer assumed as she opened her door and swung out. The Hermitage hotel was one of the most prestigious on the island although quite small. In addition to the hotel, the Group also owned several acres of land around it and three small private beaches. At Easter Andrew had told her that had the hotel been his, he would have used the land to build small holiday cottages on the same luxurious lines as those favoured in the Caribbean, and she had applauded his eager enthusiasm for his job.

As she followed Judith to the main entrance, sounds of laughter and splashing water reached her from the outdoor pool area.

'Here's the key for your room,' Judith announced ungraciously, walking behind the reception desk and removing a key which she handed to Somer, completely ignoring the other girl on reception—a newcomer since Somer's last visit. 'I'll get someone to take your stuff up.'

The casual comment did not deceive Somer for one minute. She doubted that her cases would appear in her room until Judith was good and ready to see that they did so, and another frisson of anger shook through her. Scrupulously honest herself, Somer had insisted on booking into the hotel as a guest; her room was quite an expensive one, and she had been glad of the generous cheque her father had given her a month ago to cover the cost and allow her a little extra to refurbish her wardrobe, although wisely she had left beach clothes off her list knowing that she would find a dazzlingly attractive selection in St Helier. Now Judith was treating her much in the manner of a grand lady towards a lowly governess rather than an employee to a hotel guest, but both of them knew that Somer would not complain. Even so she found the courage to say coolly, 'If you'll just tell me where I can find Andrew, I'll let him know that I'm here.'

'He'll be having his break,' Judith responded just as coolly. 'Guests aren't allowed in staff quarters. I'll leave a message for him when he comes back on duty.'

Sensing that to argue would simply demean herself, Somer took her key and walked towards the lift. Another guest was also waiting for it, a tall man dressed carelessly in faded, frayed shorts which had once been pale denim and were now bleached to a soft bluey grey by constant exposure to sun and salt. The rest of his body was bare and richly tanned and against her will Somer found her gaze drawn to the lean muscularity of it. Dark hair formed an aggressively masculine T-shape across his chest, tapering downwards to disappear beneath the faded denims.

A small sound that could have been either derision or amusement jerked her head back, the shock of cool green eyes smoothly sliding the length of her body in sensual assessment that was far more comprehensive and swift than her own bashful study of his body, jolting her into a blushing awareness that the lift had arrived and that he was waiting for her to precede him into it.

The moment the lift door closed she felt uncomfortable with their enforced intimacy. What was the matter with her, she chided herself mentally. The man lounging so easily beside her was far too physically compelling, far too masculinely attractive to need to attack women in lifts to get his sexual satisfaction. A brief darted glance at him confirmed her earlier impression of languid indolence. If she hadn't stared so foolishly at him outside the lift he would probably never even have noticed her. She had brought his brief, sexual appraisal of her down on her own shoulders.

Instinctively she knew that he was a man who would always respond to female sexuality; that he was one of those men who possess a seventh sense that enables them to tune in to a woman's response to them. He was the kind of man she could imagine appealing to the Judiths of this world. Undoubtedly sexually skilled and knowledgeable, and yet possessed of a certain basic raw masculinity that meant that despite that skill there would always be an element of subjugation that would always make him the possessor of a woman's body; the wholly dominant male.

Without knowing why she found herself taking a pace back, as though somehow he threatened her, even though he hadn't so much as moved. She could sense that he was watching her, assessing her with those incredible jade eyes, the hard-boned masculine face no doubt making no secret of his amusement at her gauche reaction.

When the lift stopped at her floor she heaved a faint sigh of relief, quickly checked when he stepped out of it behind her. The corridor seemed to stretch endlessly in front of her, her legs suddenly as shaky and unsupportive as a newly born colt's. So aware was she of his presence that she could almost feel the heat of his body against her back, wrapping her in sensual awareness, almost suffocating her, her mind a jumble of confused impressions. She found her door, and then dropped her key as she tried to insert it in the lock, tensing as she felt him stop behind her and retrieve it for her, easily sliding it into place.

When his thumb pushed aside the thick fall of her hair to rub the vulnerable spot just behind her ear she nearly jumped out of her skin, her eyes widening in shocked disbelief, so deeply violet that they were almost black.

Wicked amusement danced in jade-green depths, so deep that she could almost have drowned in them, the hard masculine mouth curling in faint derision as his thumb slid from her ear down her throat resting on the place where her pulse throbbed betrayingly.

'What on earth do you think you're doing?' Her voice, which she had wanted to sound sharp and cold, sounded breathy and faintly husky.

'Just testing to see if you actually are still wet behind the ears,' he drawled mockingly in response. 'I don't know who let you out alone without your leading reins, little girl, but they sure as hell must be worrying about you.'

To Somer's relief, he removed his fingers from her skin, although it still burned where they had been, her flesh feeling as though it were on fire. Not until she was safely inside her room with the door locked did she dare to relax, flinging herself face down on her bed and letting the tremors she had suppressed outside race violently through her. Andrew had been at first disbelieving and then faintly annoyed when she had told him that she was still a virgin. When she had questioned him about it, a little hurt to discover that he was not pleased as she had expected him to be, he had said simply that sex was more fun when one had more experience. He must have sensed her distress though because he had taken her in his arms afterwards and told her not worry about it, but comforting though his words had been, she had been left with a tiny nagging core of uncertainty. She had always assumed that the man she loved would treasure the gift of her virginity, not consider it as some sort of nuisance.

Now, alone in her room these doubts returned to plague her. Even a stranger seemed to know that she was inexperienced, 'wet behind the ears', as he had said so mockingly, with a look in his eyes that told her that he was anything but the same. For some reason as she lay on the bed it was the stranger's dark green eyes and thick black shock of hair that forced its way into her mind's eye and not Andrew's fair attractiveness.

Suddenly restless she got up and walked across to the window. She had a view of the hotel gardens; the tennis courts and swimming-pool spread out immediately below her flower-festooned balcony, and beyond it the shrubs of the natural garden and the cliff that led down to the sea, an impossible blue on this perfect summer's day.

Still feeling restless she rang room service and ordered a pot of tea, wondering when her luggage would arrive. The sight of Judith in her brief white outfit and the holidaymakers down below, enjoying themselves by the pool, made her feel dowdy in her sensible lightweight wool suit, smart enough for shopping in Aberdeen, and bought from a very good shop, but somehow out of place in her present surroundings.

When the tea arrived but her luggage still had not she rang down to reception relieved to find that Judith wasn't on duty. The girl who answered was pleasant and promised to have her cases sent straight up. Encouraged by her friendly manner Somer asked if she knew where Andrew might be found. There was a brief pause and the girl's voice changed, a faintly hesitant note entering it.

'I'm not sure,' she told Somer. 'I think he might be in the office at the moment.'

Thanking her Somer rang off. Andrew had promised that he would take a few days' holiday while she was staying at the hotel and that they could be alone together to talk over their plans. Suddenly Somer longed for him to be with her; to take her into his arms and kiss away all her doubts and fears, to obliterate completely the face of the mocking stranger who made her feel so aware of her inadequacies.

When her luggage arrived she unpacked carefully, selecting a pale lemon wrap-round skirt in cool cotton and a toning tee-shirt, which she changed into as soon as she had showered. Feeling more in keeping with the other guests she debated whether to remain in her room and wait for Andrew, or to walk through the gardens. In the event the decision was made for her. She was just finishing her second cup of tea when she heard a rap on her door.

'It's me, darling,' Andrew's familiar voice called. 'Open the door.'

'Andrew!' Her cheeks pink with excitement Somer flung herself bodily into his arms, her face raised for his kiss.

'Let me get inside.' Andrew laughed, but there was faint uneasiness in his eyes as he glanced down the empty corridor. 'I am supposed to be on duty you know.'

'I was hoping you would meet me at the airport.' They were inside the room now, but Andrew had made no move to take her back in his arms.

'Oh come on, darling, don't sulk.' Impatience edged his voice, normally so warm and loving. Tears suddenly, and appallingly, threatened, despite her efforts to blink them away. She was behaving like a child, what was wrong with her? Andrew saw the betraying sheen and was instantly apologetic.

'Darling, I'm a miserable brute, but it's just that I'm so

tired. I've had to put in extra time to make sure I could take a few days off while you're here. Forgive me for not being there, but I did send Judith, so at least you were met by a familiar face.'

Suppressing the desire to tell him that she would have been far happier with a completely strange one Somer moved back towards him. His hands cupped her shoulders, and he bent, kissing the corner of her mouth lightly, but despite the caress he was still holding her away from him and she had to suppress a feeling of disappointment. Of course he was tired, and probably the last thing he felt like was making love to her. Traitorous as a serpent the thought slithered into her mind that the stranger in the lift would never been too tired to make love, would never hold the woman he loved at arm's length when she could be moulded against his body, matching the heavy thud of his heartbeat. Quelling the thought she smiled up at Andrew, reminded herself of her recent proud boast to her father that she was grown up and adult.

'It's all right, darling,' she said softly, 'I do understand. We can talk at dinner tonight.'

His arms dropped to his sides, and he turned slightly away from her, fiddling with the lamp on the dressing-table. Her room was elegantly furnished with pretty cane furniture, its colour-scheme soft blues and greys, a soft, thick pile carpet in soft blue echoing the same colour.

'Somer, I'm sorry, I can't have dinner with you tonight. I've got a meeting on with the Manager—something I just can't get out of. Look, why don't you have something sent up to your room and get an early night. Tomorrow we can talk, make plans... You must be tired anyway after your journey.'

Somer forbode to point out that a flight of little over an hour was hardly an exhausting ordeal, meekly acceding to his suggestion and wishing the tiny nagging pain inside her would go away instead of flaring into life.

With a brief peck on her cheek Andrew left her. Feeling completely deflated, not knowing what to do with herself after the anti-climax of their reunion. Somer stared blindly out across the gardens and then glanced at her watch. It was six o'clock and the evening stretched emptily in front of her, the thought of a solitary meal in her room somehow unappealing.

Crushing the disloyal thought that suggested that Andrew might have made some time to spend with her on her very first evening, as being that of a child, not the adult she had proclaimed so vehemently to her father that she was, Somer decided that a walk through the gardens might help banish the fit of miseries that hovered threateningly.

She found that she had them almost completely to herself when she walked through the foyer and out into the open air, the pool now almost deserted, only one lone figure distorting the smooth blue water as he cleaved it with the sure overarm motions of a strong crawl. The dark head lifted just long enough for Somer to recognise the unmistakable features of the stranger from the lift, and she faltered just long enough to recognise herself and be dismayed by her own reluctance to cross the pool area in case she excited his attention for a second time in one day.

Her thoughts, as she made her way through the gardens, were all of her unsatisfactory reunion with Andrew. Her body ached with that same indefinable torment she had experienced at Easter, and she could only wonder at Andrew's greater self-control. She wanted to be married to him now, she thought rebelliously, not in nine months' time. It was all very well for her father to say that they would have the rest of their lives to spend together, but right now the nine months he had said they must wait

seemed like a lifetime. After this holiday she wouldn't see
Andrew again until Christmas. He had a month off then
and was going to spend it in Aberdeen with Somer and
her father. It would be the first time the two most important
men in her life met, and she was desperately anxious for
them to like one another.

Andrew was already predisposed to like her father, she
knew. Even when Sir Duncan had insisted that they must
wait before marrying Andrew had not lost his temper or
protested. He could understand her father's point of view,
he had admitted, and in fact he had been the one to assure
her that her father was only acting out of concern for her,
Somer remembered, thinking back to that occasion. Unfortunately she couldn't entirely escape the conviction that
her father was not equally responsive towards Andrew.
Nothing specific had been said, but she had sensed a certain lack of enthusiasm which was not entirely connected
with her age, a certain tension in her father's voice whenever she mentioned Andrew's name.

It was over an hour before she returned from her walk,
noticing as she did so that dusk was already crowding the
vividly beautiful sunset from the sky, reminding her of
how much further south Jersey was than Aberdeen where
the light nights continued well into the autumn.

Judith was back on duty on reception when Somer
walked in. She was talking to the stranger from the lift,
now dressed semi-formally in an open-throated soft white
shirt that emphasised the tanned column of his throat and
tapering black trousers which drew Somer's bemused gaze
to the leanly muscled power of his thighs. He moved
slightly as though aware of her scrutiny, even though he
couldn't possibly have seen her where she stood in the
shadows of the doorway, flexing his body slightly like a
large muscular cat taking pleasure in the fluid response of

bone and sinew. Judith followed the brief movement with admiring eyes, leaning slightly forward across the desk so that her blouse tightened revealingly across her breasts. The dark head inclined and although Somer could not see his expression, she guessed that there was an unmistakable sensual appreciation in the jade eyes as they studied the curvaceous outline of Judith's breasts.

He moved away at last, his business obviously concluded, and Somer almost shrank back into the shadows as he headed for the open main doors and out into the dusk beyond.

'Now that's what I call a man,' Judith smirked as Somer approached the desk and requested her key. 'Not that you would know what I mean. A man like that would make you run a mile wouldn't he, little scaredy-cat?'

The mocking taunt stung, and Somer grabbed for her key, colour high in her cheeks. To hide her agitation she asked huskily, 'Is he a guest here?'

'You could say that. He's Chase Lorimer, the photographer. He's been here for three weeks—working. If you can call taking pictures of bikini-clad models working.' Judith gave a softly sensual laugh. 'I must say if he was photographing me it wouldn't take him long to coax me out of my clothes and into his arms. He's all man,' she said it admiringly, 'and an extremely experienced one at that, if the gossip's anything to go by. Why the interest?' she asked, adding tauntingly, 'Surely you aren't entertaining hopes in that direction yourself? You wouldn't stand a chance, he's been besieged by beautiful women ever since he got here, and even now that his current girlfriend's gone back to London with the rest of the models, he hasn't shown any interest in anyone else. And he'd certainly never show any in a frightened little innocent like you,' she finished derisively, glancing up and down Somer's slender body. 'You just haven't got what it takes, Somer, and I doubt you ever will have. No girl who's hung on to her virginity as long as you have will ever make a man a satisfactory bed partner.'

'Andrew wants me.'

Later Somer was to ask herself what had prompted her into such a rash speech. Surely it wasn't a desire to score off on Judith; to turn the tables and make her pride sting a little.

'Does he?' Judith's smile taunted her. 'Are you sure about that, Somer? Couldn't he wait to take you in his arms the moment you got here? Are you spending tonight in his bed? Does he want you so much that he can't hide his desire for you every time he sees you. Is that how it is between the two of you?'

Her contemptuous laughter followed Somer as she fled towards the lift, each cruel word a barb biting deep into her heart. How could Judith so easily unearth her own secret fears and doubts; how could she have known of her own disquiet that Andrew had not appeared more eager to be with her; to touch her and kiss her as she was longing for him to do? Andrew respected her innocence and in-experience, she told herself, trying to calm her uneasy nerves as she headed for her room. Of course his self-control must put a strain on him; that same strain she had sensed when he walked into her room. Of course the rea-son he hadn't kissed her as she had wanted him to do was that he was concerned that their lovemaking might get out of control. Andrew was only acting out of concern for her, and it was both foolish and childish of her to wish that he would sweep her off her feet and into his bed and that he would tell her that it was impossible for him to resist the enticement of her body; that his love and desire for her were so great that he must possess her.

Thoroughly confused by her own feelings Somer opened
the door of her room, locking it firmly behind her before
going on to her small balcony, trying to will away the self-
pitying loneliness that swept her. In Aberdeen her father
would be dining with business associates as he so often
did during the week. At the weekend he was going to stay
with an old friend. They would spend it fishing, her father's favourite sport. She sighed, half wishing that her
father would marry again. She would have enjoyed having
brothers and sisters, and her father would be lonely once
she was married, but when she had broached the subject
he had told her that he had loved her mother too much to
contemplate putting someone else in her place. She hadn't
doubted that he spoke the truth, and she flushed a little
remembering her impassioned cry after she had first met
Andrew, that her father didn't understand how she felt.

'I understand all too well, lassie,' he had told her grimly.
'I can remember what it feels like to fall in love, and how
impetuous girls of eighteen can be. Your mother was that
age when I first met her, and although you were born ten
months after our marriage, you could easily have arrived
very much earlier. Some things never change,' he had concluded wryly, 'and human desire is one of them. You may
think because I'm your father that I don't understand how
you feel. It's because I do that I'm so worried for you, but
I doubt that you'll heed me any more than Catriona and I
heeded her father, although these days, things being what
they are, I suppose I needn't concern myself too much with
the possibility of an unexpected grandchild.'

That assumption on her father's part as well as driving
the rich colour to her face had brought a stumbled protest
to her lips that Somer realised with the benefit of hindsight,
had been half surprised. Had her father really believed that
she and Andrew were already lovers? From his frank state-

ments to her about his relationship with her mother it seemed plain that they had not waited for marriage before consummating their love.

Thoroughly dissatisfied with the train of her thoughts Somer decided impulsively that she had to speak to Andrew. Not now tonight when she knew he was in conference with the hotel management, but first thing tomorrow morning before his working day started. She knew where his room was, and although staff quarters were forbidden to the guests, she knew she could find her way there unnoticed. Half hidden by the clutter of thoughts milling in her brain was the hope that by taking such action she might precipitate the intimacy Andrew had previously been at pains to avoid and that seeing her in his room might urge him to forget caution and only remember their love. Her blood heated to fever pitch at the thought, her body eagerly yearning for the close proximity of his, sensations as yet only half understood coursing through her veins.

Andrew! His name was on her lips when sleep finally claimed her, but inexplicably her dreams held not Andrew's fair attractiveness, but the dark compulsion of a far different man. A man who shared Judith's contempt of her, who laughed at her and called her a silly child, even while his green eyes told her that he found nothing childish in the soft curves of her body and if he wished it he could easily take her beyond childhood and into womanhood. 'No...' She moaned the denial in her sleep, moving restlessly beneath the light quilt, trying to escape from her dreams and the threat they seemed to hold.

CHAPTER TWO

SHE was awake in plenty of time to put the previous night's plan into action. From past experience she knew that Andrew would be on duty at seven, stopping to have breakfast later in the staff dining-room, once his working day had swung into action. It was just after quarter to six when she left her room, using the stairs in preference to the lift, knowing that there were unlikely to be any other guests using them at this time of the morning and also that if she went through the fire door on the third floor it led on to the stairs to the staff bedrooms.

As she had hoped she met no one *en route* to Andrew's room, and even better his door was slightly ajar, a used tray of tea outside, suggesting that he had put it there and then forgotten to close his door.

Pushing it open gently, Somer tiptoed inside. Although much less attractively furnished than her own room, Andrew's room was pleasantly large and as she knew, doubled as a bedroom-cum-sitting room, one wall covered in units that held his books and stereo system, as well as the pull-down desk-top he used to work on, and a small portable television.

Privately she had always considered the room rather bleak, lacking a woman's touch, but as she hovered in the small hallway, her presence concealed by the door to the small bathroom, she became aware that Andrew was not alone. Her body froze as she recognised Judith's voice, husky and faintly lazy as though she were still half asleep, the small protesting sound that accompanied it quite unmistakably coming from the springs of Andrew's bed, her drawled, 'Umm, darling that was lovely,' leaving Somer in no doubt as to the intimacy she had interrupted. But worse was to come. While she hesitated like a wooden puppet, still trying to absorb the enormity of what was happening, Somer heard Judith say, 'Will you think about me while you're making love to little miss goody two-shoes?'

'Hardly.' She barely recognised Andrew's voice rich with self-satisfaction, replete with sexual pleasure, far different from the voice in which he spoke to her. 'If anything I'll think of daddy's money and the future it's going to buy for you and me one day. That's always supposing I can *bring* myself to make love to her.'

'Well, I think you're going to have to take the plunge pretty soon, my darling, otherwise she's going to get pretty suspicious. Virgin she might be, but she isn't so innocent that she doesn't know what she's missing.'

There was a brief rustling movement and then Andrew groaned, his voice strangely hoarse as he gasped out, 'Dear God, Jude, I don't know if I *can* make love to her. She turns me off completely. She hasn't got the faintest idea what to do to attract a man. If I hadn't known about daddy's money I'd never even have looked at her. It's no wonder she's still a virgin. I can't imagine any real man ever wanting her…'

The scornful words dug into Somer's heart like poison-tipped darts, unimaginable pain searing through her. She wanted to cry out her agony, to rush into the room and tear and claw at both of them. To… So no real man would want her, would he? If it was possible, knowing that Andrew thought that about her, hurt even more than the knowledge that he had only wanted her for her father's money—that she had been the victim of a cruel and greedy plot.

'Just wait until I'm married to her, then we can make plans. First a hotel in Barbados or somewhere else in the Caribbean, financed by daddy's money, and then once she realises I don't want her it shouldn't be hard to persuade her to get a divorce. The hotel will be in my name of course, and just in case daddy proves difficult there's always the threat of revealing just how inadequate his darling daughter is, if he doesn't play ball. I can just see it now, can't you? *"Oil magnate's daughter unable to arouse her husband."* No, we won't have any trouble getting rid of her when the time comes. I like a woman who's all woman, who knows how to please a man. A taste I share with our friend Lorimer, unless I'm mistaken,' Andrew added, jealousy edging under his voice, sending fresh waves of agony searing through her body.

She ought to leave before they realised that she was listening, Somer thought emptily, but the MacDonald pride would not let her, and her Celtic heritage urged her to stay and hear all that there was to hear, to endure everything there was to endure, and so she stayed where she was, opening herself to the torrent of pain sweeping over her, bowing her head beneath it with Celtic stoic acceptance of the inevitability of pain, only her fiery MacDonald pride keeping her from crying it out loud.

'Jealous,' Judith teased huskily. 'He was just chatting to me…'

'Chatting to you? Are you trying to tell me he didn't ask you out?'

'Not this time.'

'And if he did?' The jealousy in Andrew's voice increased.

'Of come on darling, you can't expect me to spend all my spare time alone while you're wining and dining Miss Oil Wells. Like you just said I'm all woman, and I have my...needs...'

Feeling physically sick Somer stepped back blindly searching for the door. She couldn't endure any more. She wouldn't endure any more and she would prove to them both that they were both wrong about her; that she could attract a man physically; that she was just as desirable as Judith, every bit as much a woman, and for starters...

Barely giving herself time to think she gathered up all her courage and walked into the room, tugging off the small diamond solitaire and tossing it bitterly on to the bed, standing in full view of both startled occupants. Judith didn't look quite as glamorous in the dawn light as she did in her full make-up, and in another half-dozen years she would begin to look blowsy, Somer decided with savage satisfaction, but it wasn't the future that concerned her now, it was the present.

'Somer!' Andrew's voice was startled and urgent, but Somer ignored it.

'Don't say a word,' she warned him bitterly, 'I've already heard enough. If I were you I'd concentrate on satisfying your...' her lip curled derisively, 'friend's "needs", that is if she still wants you now that I'm not going to provide the pair of you with a meal ticket for life. You'd got it all planned, hadn't you, but you made one vital miscalculation. I'm obviously not as frigid as you assumed, Andrew, although it's just as well I discovered the truth the way I did. I imagine it would have been very embarrassing for us both if I'd found you alone this morning. I came here hoping you would make love to me.' God how it hurt to drag out that admission, but she was going to make herself face up to just how pitiful and contempt-

ible she had been. 'But it seems you have other prefer-
ences...' She let her eyes slide dismissively over Judith's
naked shoulders, watching the rage simmer in the other
woman's eyes. 'I just hope you don't find them too expensive,' she added softly with a final flourish as she
turned towards the door.

Andrew had gone a sickly pale colour while she spoke,
but Judith was on the point of exploding with barely concealed anger. No doubt she had looked forward to a lifetime of luxury at her expense, Somer decided. She herself
must be growing up quickly because it was easy to see
that knowing she was cheating Somer must have added a
decided fillip to her affair with Andrew. Now that fillip
was gone, Judith just might turn her eyes in other directions; she even found herself hoping that she might, and
that Andrew, who was plainly besotted with her, would
suffer as she was now suffering.

Somer thought she would die with the mortification of
it. Was there something wrong with her? Some vital element lacking? Something that made her less feminine than
other women, some deep female core that was simply
missing from her make up. 'No!' The denial was torn from
her throat and prompted her headlong flight from the scene
of her humiliation. All her fierce MacDonald pride rose up
inside her, a look in her eyes that her father would have
recognised, her wild untamed Highland blood crying out
for vengeance, for balm to soothe her aching pride. She
had loved and tasted the bitter dregs of betrayal, she would
never touch either again. But first she had to make good
her initial promise to herself.

Not stopping to analyse her reaction to the scene she
had just experienced Somer hurried on, knowing only that
to remain still was to open herself to the same pain which
had overwhelmed her in Andrew's bedroom. Her first in-

stinct to flee, to simply leave the hotel and go home, was lost beneath the tidal swell of a need to prove Andrew and Judith's cruel comments wrong. She would find a man who wanted her and she would find him before her holiday was over.

Down in the foyer she saw that Judith was just about to take over the reception desk. Another girl, a stranger to Somer, was talking to one of the hotel guests, his broad shoulders bent towards her. Somer felt her heartbeat accelerate as she recognised the male outline of him. A real man, Judith had called Chase Lorimer; a very sensual man Somer would have called him; a man who would not think twice about taking what he wanted from life, a man who would teach her in one lesson far more about the game of love than a thousand fumbling encounters with boys as inexperienced as she was herself. Half a dozen steps away from the desk Somer halted. She could hear him asking the way to a small little-known local cove. The girl behind the reception desk frowned.

'I'm sorry, Mr Lorimer,' Somer heard her apologise, 'I'm afraid I don't know where it is, but if you'll just bear with me for a moment I'll try to find out.' She glanced round to Judith who was deep in conversation with Andrew and Somer reacted blindly, urged on by the same fierce MacDonald pride which had buoyed her up earlier.

A little to her own surprise she heard herself saying coolly, 'I know where the cove is.' She saw Andrew's head jerk up in recognition of her voice. 'In fact...' Chase Lorimer had turned round and was surveying her with that same lazy scrutiny she recognised from the previous day. 'In fact I was planning to go there myself today. Perhaps we could travel there together? Do you have a car?'

'Yes, how long will it take us to get there?'

Somer breathed shakily, unaware of how tense she had

been until she heard him speak. There was only the cool anonymity of his voice to go on, and that did not give her any clues as to his reaction to her invitation. 'Half an hour,' she responded nervously.

Of course in the world he inhabited it was probably quite normal for women to issue the invitations; certainly he didn't seem shocked or surprised that she had done so, his lounging stance by the reception desk barely altered as he turned to glance at her.

'Can you be ready in an hour?' He glanced at his watch. 'I normally have a swim before breakfast, and then we can meet down here when you're ready.'

Out of the corner of her eye Somer could see Judith's stunned, almost bitter expression, but she kept her own features unreadable as she acquiesced. So Chase Lorimer swam every morning; no doubt that explained what he was doing in the foyer so early, well before any of the other guests had put in an appearance.

Confirming their arrangements, Somer headed back to her own room to change her clothes and pack a bag to take with her, a fierce elation filling her. For once the fates seemed disposed to be on her side, and she derived a considerable amount of satisfaction from the looks she had seen on Andrew's and Judith's faces when Chase Lorimer accepted her invitation. She had just reached the lift when Judith slipped up behind her, tapping her contemptuously on the arm.

'It won't work, you know,' she hissed tauntingly. 'Oh, you might have forced Chase Lorimer to accept your company for a couple of hours but he'll never take you to bed, not once he discovers the truth about you. Men like him don't go for virgins, especially not plain, uninteresting ones like you. He's a photographer, and rumour has it that every time he makes love to a woman he takes her photograph—for his own private collection.'

Somer battled against a sudden feeling of revulsion which pierced her newly won armour long enough for her to regret the impetuosity of what she had done, but with the next breath Judith swept aside her doubts, her voice mocking as she drawled, 'Anyway, even if you did get him to take you to bed, it won't make any difference to the way Andrew feels about you. It won't make him jealous if that's what you're thinking. Andrew loves me.'

'Does he?' Somer was amazed at the cool control of her voice. 'Funny, I had the impression that his first love was money, and as for making him jealous, I wouldn't bother wasting my time. In fact seeing the two of you together has made it all much easier for me. I think I realised I'd made a mistake about Andrew, the moment I...'

'Set eyes on Chase Lorimer?' Judith suggested sneeringly. 'For such an innocent you certainly know how to recognise quality goods when you see them, but Chase Lorimer won't be interested in daddy's money. He's got a wealthy uncle of his own, and Chase is his sole heir.'

'You seem to know a great deal about him. Did you have designs on him yourself?'

The lift door opened just as Judith raised her hand, and Somer stepped smartly into it, leaving the other girl outside. As she pressed the button for her floor she sank back against the metal wall, trying to compose herself. Her legs felt as weak as jelly, her breathing uneven. She had never in her life participated in the kind of row she had just had with Judith and it left a sour taste in her mouth. So Chase Lorimer photographed the women he made love to, did he? She shivered suddenly, stumbling out of the lift when it reached her floor. It isn't too late to turn back, a tiny inner voice urged her, but to turn back meant admitting that every humiliating insult Judith and Andrew had thrown at her was true; that she didn't have what it took to be a real woman, and she was determined to prove them wrong.

In her room she riffled through her suitcase until she found what she was looking for, a bikini she had bought in the south of France the previous summer when she was on holiday with Claire. Claire had persuaded her to buy it, and she had only worn it once, scandalised by the brevity of the pink and black striped cotton fabric. She tried it on in front of her mirror, refusing to flinch away from the sight of her barely clad body. The triangles of fabric that tied in bows over her hips revealed the slender length of her legs and far more of her than Scottish prudence thought wise, but how could she expect Chase Lorimer to take the bait unless it was presented to him temptingly? she asked herself with a sudden new cynicism. Judith wouldn't have wavered for a moment and, in fact, would probably have dispensed with the top half of the bikini altogether. As Judith had told her Chase Lorimer was a man used to the company of beautiful women; he was also a man who was probably not used to a celibate existence, even for a short period of time, and he was alone at the hotel, now that the models had returned to London.

Carefully packing her beach bag with oil, towels, a paperback and other bits and pieces Somer firmly refused to listen to the tiny corner of her mind still pleading sanity, telling herself that there might never be an opportunity like this again. If she failed with Chase Lorimer... But she would not fail. He was a man who needed women and the look in his eyes yesterday had told her, despite everything that Judith and Andrew had said, that he had been interested enough to study her carefully.

Pulling on a pale pink cotton top and matching shorts,

and throwing a casual button-through dress into her bag, Somer slipped on her mules, and headed for the door. A glance at her watch confirmed that she still had fifteen minutes to go before she was due to meet Chase. Just enough time to have a cup of coffee in the Continental coffee shop on the ground floor of the hotel.

Somer ordered a cup of coffee and some toast, trying to stem the growing protest of her nerves as the minutes ticked by. Eight o'clock came and went, and perspiration broke out on her skin. He wasn't coming. He had changed his mind. She wanted to be sick, and kept imagining Judith's gloating face. She had a good view of the foyer from where she was sitting, and she could see everyone who came in or left.

At ten past eight she conceded defeat. No doubt he had never meant to meet her, and had merely agreed out of politeness. Sick with humiliation and misery, Somer searched feverishly through her bag and withdrew her small make-up mirror, flicking it open to scrutinise her too-pale features and tell-tale bruised eyes. A surreptitious glance into the foyer assured her that at least Judith wasn't there to witness her humiliation, although no doubt she would get to know about it and she and Andrew would laugh about it together. Too engrossed in the bitterness of her thoughts to hear the footsteps approaching. Somer tensed in shock as she felt the cool drift of lean fingers against her arm, whirling round, white-faced to confront the inscrutable features of Chase Lorimer.

'So this is where you're hiding. Have you forgotten about our date?'

He had changed into slim fitting off-white jeans, a black shirt open at the throat, the sleeves rolled back. A gold watch glinted through the dark hair on his arm, and Somer had the sudden panicky impression of a man who for all the trappings of modern-day sophistication was as much a pirate in his way as the inhabitants of this particular stretch of Jersey coastline had once been.

'I...I hadn't forgotten. I just didn't see you in the foyer.'

'I've just been out to put some petrol in the car, that's why I'm a few minutes late. This yours?' He picked up her bag, and stood waiting for her to join him, and Somer knew that now it was too late to listen to all those warning voices she had ignored so strenuously earlier on.

'I hope you've brought plenty of suntan cream,' he warned her. 'I've been told that this particular cove is a sun-trap and quite remote. There's no shop or cafe there.'

Did his warning hold another meaning? The suggestion that perhaps he regretted allowing her to come with him and that he would prefer to spend the day alone? As Somer knew from past experience, the path down to the beach was narrow and in places almost unsafe. She had gone there at Easter with Andrew, and although it had been a pleasant, warm day, she had come back feeling edgy and yes, disappointed. Because Andrew hadn't made any attempt to make love to her, she acknowledged, filled with bitter resentment again. The cove was an almost idyllic place for lovers; secluded; sheltered, not overlooked by houses or roads.

'Here we are.' She came to an abrupt halt as Chase Lorimer stopped beside a gleaming black Porsche with the top folded back. 'Are you going to wear your hat, or shall I put it in the boot?'

'I...in the boot please,' Somer mumbled handing it over to him and then snatching her fingers back as though they had been burned the moment they came into contact with his. It had been the briefest contact imaginable and yet she had shied away from it like a...like a terrified virgin, she castigated herself mentally. How on earth did she expect him to make love to her when she recoiled from even the slightest physical contact with him?

'I've had the hotel pack us up some lunch. I take it you do plan to spend most of the day there? There's no public transport there…'

And by inviting herself to join him as his guide, she had also invited herself to be his companion for the day, or as much of it as he chose to share with her, Somer acknowledged. 'I'm in your hands completely,' she responded daringly, holding her breath and looking away when she felt him move towards her, but he stretched past her, opening the passenger door, and she slid inside the car on shaky legs, wondering if there was ever going to come a time when she felt completely at ease in the company of men like Chase Lorimer, able to flirt and tease them in the way that seemed second nature to the Judiths and Claires of this world.

'It all depends how long it takes me to take the photographs I need,' Chase told her as he slid into his own seat and slipped on a pair of sunglasses. 'I want to take some background shots to use in the studio, just in case any of the work I've already done doesn't work out. Ready?'

Somer nodded, carefully giving him instructions as to their route as he turned out on to the road that led away from the hotel.

'Left here, is it?' he checked once they gained the main road. Somer nodded, her hand going up to secure her hair, already thoroughly tousled from their short drive. If she'd known he was driving an open-topped car she would have tied it back with a ribbon, but it was too late to do anything about it now, other than to try and keep it out of her eyes.

'Leave it,' Chase ordered softly when she made another bid to capture the errant strands. 'With it loose and tousled like that you look the epitome of wanton innocence. Is it naturally that colour?'

'Yes.' Somer's cheeks stung with bright colour.

'No need to look so outraged, most models tint theirs, these days, and it isn't often you see someone with true blue-black hair and such a pale skin. Coupled with your eyes, I'd say that was a Celtic heritage, Irish perhaps?'

'Scots,' she corrected him briefly. This man knew far too much about her sex, far, far too much, and she shivered slightly despite the growing heat of the sun. What had she committed herself to? Why had she allowed her fiendish MacDonald pride to hold sway the way she had? She had been warned on many occasions by her father to treat the MacDonald curse carefully, but she had ignored him, and now she was seated in this car with this stranger heading for a remote beach where she had planned that he would make love to her.

What was the matter with her? Was she really going to back out now? Coward, coward, an inner voice mocked her. You haven't got the guts to go through with it. I have, Somer gritted mentally, I have got the guts and I shall, I shall.

'You're looking very serious, something on your mind? Second thoughts about spending the day with me perhaps?'

Somer glanced in shocked response into Chase's shuttered face. His sunglasses hid his expression from her, her heart pounding in frightened reaction to his astute perception.

'No...'

'You don't sound very sure. Don't worry about it, whatever you might have heard to the contrary, I don't go in for rape. I don't need to,' he told her wryly, 'and now that we've got that out of the way how about telling me what you're doing here on holiday alone.'

'I…I was going to come with my boyfriend, but…but we had a row and…'

'And now you're looking for a substitute,' he suggested drily. 'Well why not? Strange, from the tragic look on your face earlier this morning, I thought the roof had fallen in on you at least. You looked like a tormented lost kitten whom someone had kicked once too often,' he mocked, smiling into her pale, stunned face.

'You felt sorry for me?' Somer blurted out. 'Is that why…'

'I let you pick me up?' he offered, smiling sardonically at her. 'Not entirely, I'm no altruist. If you'd been forty and plain I dare say I wouldn't have felt anything like as sympathetic. I suppose I should have guessed it was all down to some man. You're just the right age for emotional hysterics, aren't you? How old are you?'

'Eighteen.' She didn't even consider lying, but flinched when his fingers tightened momentarily on the steering wheel and he murmured mock piously, 'Dear God, as young as that. I'm twenty-eight—a whole generation older—or are you going to tell me you prefer older men?'

'My tastes are pretty catholic,' Somer retorted, her chin jutting defiantly under his mockery. 'In everything.'

There was a moment's silence, and when he glanced at her again there was no humour etched against the curling mouth, only a grim appreciation of her closing remark.

'Is that so?' he drawled. 'Well then it looks like we're going to have an enlightening day. I would have thought that eighteen wasn't old enough to have tasted all the pleasures life has to offer, but it seems that I'm wrong, and a girl like you wouldn't be short of tutors. That pseudo air of innocence must have deceived more than one member of my sex in the past. How many lovers have you had, just as a matter of interest, or don't you bother to count any longer?'

Half appalled by the direction the conversation had taken, Somer reminded herself that to tell the truth at this stage would probably wreck all her plans. Her mouth opened and almost without her having to think about it, she was saying flippantly, 'Why do you want to know? Are you hoping to become one of them?' She had a moment in which to be horrified by the cheap provocation of her remark and then Chase was saying smoothly, 'So that's your game, is it? Well, time alone will tell, won't it? You know the odds better than I do, and you've got all day to persuade me that it might be worth my while, haven't you?'

'Turn right here,' Somer interrupted shakily. The conversation had taken a turn she had never envisaged, but surely the fates were playing into her hands once again in allowing her to deceive Chase Lorimer into believing that she was sexually experienced, and that by inviting herself to spend the day with him, she was inviting him to make love to her?

But for how long could she continue to deceive him? Cold reality intruded. Surely he would know the minute he touched her that she had been lying? Was she trying to give herself an excuse to back out again, the voice of her MacDonald pride demanded relentlessly. Didn't she have the guts to go through with it?

They were driving down a narrow country lane, empty of traffic, a dazzling blue carpet melting into the horizon in the distance.

Directing Chase from memory, Somer heaved a faint sigh of relief when they turned into the small car park at the top of the cliff. The path she remembered was indicated by a small gate in the perimeter of the dusty clifftop.

'Just how steep is this path?' Chase asked when they were out of the car.

'Very,' Somer told him.

'Umm, then I'd better make two journeys. I don't want to risk damaging my camera, but at least we should have the place to ourselves, if it's as inaccessible as all that. Not the spot to take the kids, I take it?'

'Not unless they're the four-legged variety,' Somer responded humorously, catching the mobile lift of his eyebrows as Chase registered her comment.

'A sense of humour as well. My, my, things are looking up. Can you manage your own stuff, or…?'

'I can manage it.'

'Ah yes, I forgot you're a product of a new generation aren't you; a girl who probably imbibed liberation with her mother's milk. Just as a matter of interest, what do your parents think of your present life-style?'

'My mother's dead,' Somer said shortly, 'and my father…'

'Is an ex-sixties hippy who approves of free love and has brought up his daughter to share his views. Well, who am I to complain?' He shrugged broad shoulders and went to the boot of the car, levering it open.

'Here you are. You can start down if you like, I'll get my stuff together. Gorgeous day,' he added, stretching with the same languorous movement she had noticed the previous day. 'You'll have to watch that skin of yours. You'll find a bad case of sunburn will cramp your style very effectively.'

Her face flushed, Somer grabbed her bag from him and headed for the cliff. The hot weather had dried out the path, clouds of dust and small pebbles were disturbed by her steady progression downwards. Several times she had to grab hold of tussocks of grass to prevent herself from falling and when she eventually reached the small cove Somer let out a sigh of relief.

The cove was every bit as attractive as she remembered, guarded on three sides by the cliffs and on the fourth by the sea. There was no one else in sight, the sand smooth and unmarked, the tide lapping gently at the soft golden sand. Slipping off her mules Somer let her toes curl luxuriously into the sun-warmed fine grains, feeling the tension ease out of her as she breathed in the clear, fresh air, only to tense up again as she heard sounds of movement behind her, and turned just in time to see Chase depositing several pieces of equipment on a small tarpaulin behind her.

'Umm, we really have got the place to ourselves, haven't we,' he commented as he headed back for the path. 'I shan't be long—why don't you make yourself comfortable while I'm gone?' he mocked her. 'I'm sure a free-thinking, modern liberationist like yourself feels more at home on the nudist beaches of the continental holiday resorts than the family ones of Jersey, but no one's going to see you if you strip off here. I might even join you.'

With his last threat ringing in her ears, Somer turned her back on him, leaving him to return to his car while she wandered over to the tide-line, watching the small waves lapping at the sand, gradually receding as the tide went out.

By the time Chase finally returned from his second journey, her nerves were coiled as tightly as an overwound spring and she was bitterly regretting her foolhardiness in coming with him, but something stronger than her fear, stronger than her natural reluctance to experiment with what every instinct told her should be a beautiful and precious moment in her life, not something done in anger and a mood of bitter resentment, overrode everything else, urging her to stick to her original plan drowning out all her other warning voices clamouring for attention, telling her that she must seize the moment and make the most of it.

Almost defiantly she retraced her footsteps along the beach, coming to a standstill several feet away from Chase's equipment. He was standing with his back to her, opening a zipped bag from which he removed a towel, dropping it on the beach, and then glancing at his watch. 'I can't do any work for a couple of hours yet, the angle of the sun isn't right. I'm going for a swim, want to join me?'

'Not yet. I want to sunbathe first.'

His hand went to the buttons on his shirt, casually flicking them open, whilst Somer watched, almost transfixed, only able to draw her eyes away when the mat of dark hair shadowing his skin was finally revealed. A curious sensation of weakness swept over her, and she shivered, suddenly caught up in a mental vision of what it would be like to feel Chase's body against her own; to smooth her fingertips through that dark arrowing of hair, her naked breasts pressed close to his skin. She closed her eyes, and then opened them again to find that Chase had removed both shirt and jeans and was standing in front of her, studying her with a frown, his only covering a brief pair of swimming shorts, the white fabric contrasting starkly with his deep tan. His body was as leanly muscular as she had imagined, but far more sleekly powerful, the sight of it sending frissons of awareness shuddering through her as she felt the power of his raw masculinity.

She watched him lope down to the water's edge and beyond until he was swimming strongly away from her. Only then did she drag her eyes away from the clean lines of his body, her fingers trembling as she pulled off her tee-shirt and shorts to reveal the scanty bikini she was wearing underneath.

She had just finished carefully anointing her skin with suntan lotion when Chase came striding towards her. Moisture glinting on his skin, tiny droplets running down over his chest, tangling in the dark hair. He raised one hand, smoothing his tangled hair back off his forehead, and grinned down at her, his eyes narrowing as he took in the brevity of her bikini, coming to stand over her, making her feel like a slave girl cowering before the pirate who had stolen her away.

A droplet of water splashed from his arm on to the vulnerable skin between her breasts making her jump. Almost instantly the jade eyes darkened and Chase bent down, swift as a hawk to the lure, his tongue brushing roughly against the curves of her breasts as it dipped into the valley between and found the errant drop of moisture. At the touch of his tongue a thousand emotions assailed her; her body both hot and cold at the same time, tense and feverish as she tried to assimilate her response to his brief caress.

'You're trembling.' His fingers cupped the shoulder nearest to him and he lifted his head to frown.

'I...it was just the cold water,' Somer lied, knowing she was abandoning her last opportunity to draw back and tell him the truth. 'It made me shiver.'

'Umm. You're all goosebumps.' His thumb trailed lightly down the tender underside of her arm, increasing the frissons of awareness racing under her skin. 'Why don't you take this off? After all there's no one to see but me.' His free hand tugged at the straps of her bikini top, gently pulling them loose.

'No...I...I don't want to burn,' Somer protested, knowing with fatalistic intuition that he wasn't going to listen to her as his fingers found the front fastening of her bikini and easily unclipped it. His eyes held hers in some sort of magnetic spell as his fingers brushed aside the brief triangles of cotton and his hands, warm and slightly work-roughened, cupped the smooth fullness of her breasts.

'Umm. Nice.' His fingers spanned the full warmth of her, the intimacy of his touch stealing away her breath and making her heart pound frantically. Chase freed one breast, his eyes never leaving her face as he reached for her discarded suntan lotion, slowly uncapping it. 'Put some in my hand,' he ordered softly. Panic seared through her, and she struggled against both it and a craven impulse to push his hand away and cover her breasts from him. 'What do you want it for?' How breathy, and in some way provocative her voice sounded, almost unfamiliar to her own ears.

'I'm going to make sure you don't burn,' he returned lazily. 'Isn't that what you wanted?'

A thousand denials sprang to mind, but he was watching her too closely. Somer moistened her dry lips, flicking round them with the tip of her tongue, startled by the way his pupils dilated following the brief movement. Having gone so far it would be folly to pull back now. This was what she wanted, she reminded herself, but somehow she had just never envisioned this particular intimacy. She had wanted Chase to make love to her but...

Too confused to deal lucidly with all the conflicting emotions rioting through her she weakly did as he asked, pouring some of the creamy lotion into his open palm, and then watching like someone hypnotised as he transferred the cream to her breast, smoothing it in with long, languorous stokes that explored and moulded the shape of her, slowly circling her breast until she was aware of nothing apart from the knowing touch of his fingers. A tight coiling feeling built up inside her; an awareness of her breasts she had never known before, her nipples tingling and aching in a way that was both alien and frightening, the soft pink aureoles springing to life in a way that was openly provocative.

'No wonder so many of my sex have found you irresistible,' Chase marvelled huskily, his eyes no longer on her face but resting instead on the quivering peaks he was still anointing. 'This...' his thumb brushed lightly over one tormentingly erect nipple, 'is incitement enough for a saint, never mind a mere male. I had planned to sunbathe a little myself, but perhaps another cold dip is more in order.' He squeezed more lotion into his other hand, reaching towards her as he knelt at her side, lowering his head towards her breast.

Somer closed her eyes in mute agony at the first brush of his tongue against her nipple, waves of shame coursing through her at the first wanton stirrings of response springing to life inside her. This was something she had not bargained for. She wanted to lose her virginity but she had never dreamed she would feel like this; that she would experience this stomach-twisting, yearning need to arch blindly beneath the rough lash of his tongue; to capture his dark head and hold it against her breast, savouring the pleasure that was almost pain as his tongue ceased its torment and his lips took its place tugging gently until she was lost in a feverish surge of pleasure that breached every virginal defence.

'Later,' Chase muttered as he released her breast and lifted himself away from her. 'I've got work to do. Remember?'

Flushed and feverish, aching with tormenting desire Somer could only stare up at him, appalled by what was happening to her. She had desired Andrew of course, but that desire was a tepid, insignificant emotion when compared with what she had just experienced. The hot sun heated her skin as Chase drew away, and far from wanting to cover her breasts any more, Somer admitted that she wanted him to look at her; to desire her; to touch her and kiss her until she felt that pulsing, jerky pleasure pound through her body.

'Don't look at me like that,' Chase warned huskily, his voice intruding on her private daydream. 'You look like an innocent girl who's just discovered the magic of sex and wants to learn more. Much, much more.'

'I am and I do.' The admission hovered on her lips only to be forced back. What good would it do now to admit that she was a virgin? Chase would probably turn from her in disgust just as Andrew had done. Scarcely admitted, but there at the back of her mind was the knowledge that she no longer wanted him to make love to her simply because she wanted to rid herself of the burden of her virginity. She wanted him as well. As Chase moved away she arched seductively back on her towel, knowing with some deep feminine instinct that his eyes would be drawn to the full curves of her breasts still taut from his lovemaking. As he started to turn away she ran her hand lightly up over her body, her eyes slumberous and heavy with desire.

'Try and tempt me, would you?' Chase growled. 'Well, there's a cure for that.'

Before she could stop him he scooped her up in his arms, striding out into the sea with her, until he was standing chest high in the waves.

Somer shrieked protestingly as he let her go, startled by the impact of the cold sea water against her skin, but swimming away as agilely as an eel once she had recovered from the shock. She had learned to swim almost before she could walk and was used to the cold water of the North Sea. As she swam away Chase came after her, grabbing her ankle and tugging her down below the water, following her up to the surface, his hands grasping her waist as he pulled her hard against him, stroking her mouth with his tongue. 'Mmm. You taste of salt.'

'So do you,' Somer responded daringly, letting her own tongue repeat the caress and then breaking away to swim back to the shore. Chase didn't follow her, and gradually as she watched him Somer felt her pulse-rate subside to normal.

He followed her on to the beach five minutes later, and lay down beside her on his towel, letting the sun dry the moisture from his skin, but not making any move to touch her.

Suddenly sleepy after the physical exercise and mental strain of the morning Somer rolled over on to her stomach, burying her face in her hands. Gradually she felt the tension easing out of her body. She closed her eyes, dimly aware of firm sure hands moving over her back, inducing a delicious sensation of lethargy that made her want to stretch and curl her body like a small cat, but before she could do so sleep claimed her.

Finishing his self-imposed task Chase Lorimer studied the female form stretched out beside him. Very, very enticing; there had been a moment earlier on when he had come dangerously close to losing his self-control. He had thought the first time he saw her in the lift that she was still a child, shy and nervous. How wrong he had been! He grimaced faintly to himself. He ought to be used to it by now; after all she wouldn't be the first female to pick him up thinking she was taking the first step up the ladder to becoming a top model. A touch of contempt darkened his eyes, his expression faintly bleak. Funny, but this time it really hurt.

Shrugging mentally he got to his feet, telling himself sardonically that he was a fool to let himself get involved, but he knew he wanted her; against all logic and common sense maybe, but still he wanted her. But before he took her he would lay it on the line for her, tell her that no way was making love with him the equivalent of the modelling world's casting couch. He frowned as he glanced down at her. Lying like that with her head pillowed in her arms she looked like a child, innocent, untouched. He grimaced faintly. He was getting far too sentimental, surely life with Laura had taught him that. He had believed himself in love with her and her with him, but all she had wanted was to use him. She had laughed at him when he proposed marriage, and inflicted a painful blow to his twenty-two-year-old ego, but the tables were turned now; now that she was a fading star, a model who was finding it more and more difficult to get assignments, who needed all the tricks a clever photographer could use to preserve the illusion of youth; who at thirty betrayed in her face the way she had lived—and loved, if you could call the casual sexual encounters she indulged in, that. Now Laura wanted to marry him, especially now that she knew that he was his uncle's heir, but he wasn't twenty-two any longer; he had grown older and wiser; there had been far too many Lauras in his life for him to be deceived.

As he glanced down at Somer again his eyes were tinged with sadness and a hint of self-contempt, and here was another. A potential Laura, young enough to have the bloom still on her skin and the illusion of innocence but in reality… Picking up his equipment he headed for one end of the beach and soon became engrossed in his self-imposed task, glancing up only once to stare at the sleeping figure.

CHAPTER THREE

IT WAS the chink of a bottle against glass that brought Somer out of her light sleep, her eyes hazy with uncertainty. The sun was hot on her bare shoulders, its angle in the sky telling her how long she had slept—payment for her inability to do so properly last night.

'Good, you're awake, I was just thinking I would have to eat my lunch alone. Are you hungry?'

A picnic hamper was open on a towel next to him, and Somer peered into it, trying to suppress the agitation prickling her skin. Had she been completely mad? she wondered muzzily. Had she really intended to...to seduce this dark, arrogant stranger into making love to her? She jumped when Chase reached across and touched her shoulder, his eyebrows drawn together in a frown.

'You're not suffering from sunstroke, are you?' he queried, letting his fingers absorb the heat from her skin. 'I did cream your back for you but you have been lying there for a couple of hours.'

'I'm feeling fine,' she lied brazenly, bending her head over the wicker basket so that he couldn't see the faint tell-tale flush on her skin. 'I just couldn't remember where I was when I first woke up.'

'Or who you were with,' Chase supplemented drily, 'but then I suppose you're used to that. Pass me something to eat, will you, while I pour the wine.'

Two plates of chicken salad were attractively arranged

under a protective film, and investigating the basket further Somer discovered crusty French bread, salmon pâté, and some Brie. In one corner of the basket were peaches and grapes, and the appetite she had lacked earlier suddenly made her feel quite hungry. She handed Chase his plate, trying not to recoil from the brief brush of his fingers against hers.

'More wine?'

Somer glanced into her glass surprised to see that she had almost drained it.

'Please.' She was thirsty and besides wasn't alcohol supposed to have a relaxing effect on the nervous system?

They ate in silence with Somer stealing brief, nervous glances at Chase's inscrutable face, her eyes sliding against her will to the broad expanse of his chest with its fine covering of dark hair, and lower, almost hypnotised by that same arrowing of hair over his body.

As he bent to replenish her glass for the third time Chase mocked softly, 'You're looking at me as though I'm the first man you've ever seen, and it's having a highly combustible effect on my nervous system.'

'I wasn't looking at you, I was thinking,' Somer lied protestingly, hanging her head so that he wouldn't see her betraying blush.

'About touching me instead of merely looking at me,' Chase agreed. 'You were looking at me like a little girl let loose inside a toyshop.'

'I've told you I was miles away,' Somer protested hotly. 'I'm sorry if you thought I was staring at you...'

'Why get so het up about it? I'm flattered. Or isn't that part of the game? Does the man have to let you know how hungry he is for you before you'll deign to admit you want him in return?'

Somer could only stammer, 'No...I...I don't want you.'

'No?' Just for a second she had a brief glimpse of something fiercely bitter burning in the depths of his eyes and then it was caged, his voice urbanely amused as he reached out and stroked his thumb across her chin. 'Peach juice,' he murmured when she shied away. His fingers curled along her jaw holding her captive, and Somer felt her breath explode in a tight knot inside her chest as he bent his head, his tongue touching her skin as he licked away the small trickle of juice.

Every nerve in her body seemed to lock, and yet at the same time a wild fluttery excitement pulsed through her, her dazed eyes holding the impenetrable gaze of the dark green ones now close enough for her to see their tiny gold specks like a dusting of gold in jade malachite.

A dizzying sensation swept through her and she clutched automatically at Chase's arm to prevent herself from overbalancing. Beneath her fingers his muscles tensed and then relaxed, his maurauding tongue stroking hypnotically along the tremulous line of her mouth.

As though they were weighed down with lead weights Somer felt her eyelids dropping, a delicious languorous pleasure stealing through her. Deep inside her warning bells clamoured for attention but she felt too pleasurably relaxed to pay any attention to them. Her head swam faintly, her mind muzzy from the wine she had drunk. When Chase pushed her back on her towel Somer murmured a soft protest, but her fingers still clung to his arms, and every time she tried to open her eyes the world whirled round dizzyingly. No, it was much easier and pleasanter to simply lie here and enjoy the soft drift of Chase's hands over her skin, stroking her throat, tracing her collar bone. When he removed the top of her bikini she murmured a small protest, but his mouth stifled the sound almost at birth.

'Open your mouth. I want to taste all the sweetness of you, Somer.' Too bemused to obey Somer kept her lips pressed together, anxiety briefly piercing her alcohol-induced haze. Her muzzy brain reminded her that she had sworn that no one would ever be able to mock her inexperience again.

'Somer, stop teasing me.' Chase's voice, hoarsely impatient, shivered through her, his teeth nipped at her lower lip, her small cry of pain swallowed up as his tongue gained the access it had been seeking.

Waves of shivering excitement thudded through her, her senses totally bemused by the total seduction of Chase's mouth against her own. She could feel the heavy beat of his heart against her skin, urging her pulses to match its heady urgency.

'Somer.' Slowly Chase lifted his mouth from hers, rasping her name, twining his fingers in her hair as his lips traced the vulnerable curve of her throat closing over the pulse beating so wildly at its base.

Something wild and pagan seemed to have taken over her body, Somer thought dazedly, there could be no other explanation for the surge of response sweeping through her; the almost primaeval reaction of her body to his touch, as though all her life-forces flooded to the point where his mouth absorbed the texture of her skin.

When he lifted his head dark patches of colour stained his high cheekbones, his eyes almost black as he muttered hoarsely, 'You make me want to do things no woman has ever made me want to do before. I want to absorb you completely into me, to possess you in such a way that you're part of me for ever.' His voice, thick and slurred, touched some deep part of her consciousness making her body shiver in his arms, the fingers covering the pulse in her throat registering the shattering impact his words had on her.

'Tell me you want me the same way, Somer,' Chase groaned into the valley between her breasts. 'Tell me you feel the same spell; the same need.'

As though his hunger was too great to allow finesse lean fingers cupped her breast, and Somer felt the shudder that rippled through his body as Chase let his tongue seek its soft pink peak. His heartbeats thudded against her like a sledgehammer, pleasure piercing her; exploding inside her as she felt the rough caress of his tongue against her nipple. 'Somer,' he muttered her name with a thick raw hunger, that pierced through her alcoholic daze, panic racing through her as she felt the heat coming off his body, and its fine tremble against her as he muttered something unintelligible, the words buried in his throat, his mouth closing over the aroused crown of her breast.

Panic was forgotten as Somer gave in to the violent tide of feeling coiling through her body. Any type of lucid thought was totally impossible, her slender frame responding convulsively to Chase's heated suckling.

'Somer, you're a witch, do you know that?' Chase groaned rawly against her skin. His free hand caressed her hip; found the barrier of her bikini briefs, his fingers tugging impatiently at the confining bows.

'Somer, I want you so badly. Help me...touch me.'

Her fingers were curled into his shoulders and she tensed, trembling as he reached up and released one hand. 'Why are you tormenting me like this?' His tongue found her open palm and caressed it with rough warmth making her shiver with the weakness that invaded her body. 'Make love to me,' Chase urged huskily, his breath warm against her skin. 'Can't you see how hungry I am for your touch?'

He tugged gently on her hand placing it on his hip and

Somer trembled, acutely aware of the warmth of his skin and the bone and muscle it clothed. He moved, the dark hair on his chest and legs faintly abrasive against her tender skin, and yet it was an abrasion that hinted at pleasure. Feeling as though she were teetering on the edge of a precipice Somer closed her eyes and let her fingers explore the alien male shape of him, moving upwards over his flat stomach, tracing the arrowing of dark hair and feeling the contraction of his ribs as he breathed in sharply, trapping her fingers against his skin.

'So you *do* feel it too.' There was fiercely male exultation in the words. 'You want me as much as I want you, so stop tormenting us both, Somer. Take me inside you. You must know how much I ache to be there.'

His body shuddered and he pulled her against his body, letting her know the extent of his arousal. It shocked Somer into brief awareness of what she was doing; of the fact that she was lying naked in the arms of a man who was virtually a stranger and that she was there because she wanted to lose her virginity; and that he thought... She shuddered, forcing herself to face up to what Chase thought. He thought she was as experienced as he was himself and that she was simply not touching him to tease him, but the truth was that she daren't touch him; that the maleness of his body excited and alarmed her, and yet somewhere deep inside her she knew with a knowledge too deeply embedded to be denied that this was the man she wanted as her first lover; that something fierce and elemental in him called out to her own core of femininity and that her body responded to him in a way that had nothing to do with the emotions Andrew had aroused in her. Sexual chemistry, she told herself bleakly. That's all it was, sheer sexual chemistry, more potent and far more dangerous by a million degrees than she had ever dreamed in the days when she had smugly mentally criticised her peers for giving in to it.

'Somer.' Chase's voice was hoarse, his face suddenly frighteningly familiar.

'But you haven't photographed me yet.' She pouted the words up at him, amazed to hear them leave her lips, amazed at her own ability to play for time. She saw his expression and said provocatively, 'I thought you always photographed the women you made love to.'

'So I was right, that's what this is all about.' His expression changed so quickly it was frightening. One minute he was a passionate lover, the next a cold-eyed stranger. 'I suppose I ought to have known. Well, you don't have the body to make a model,' he told her disparagingly. 'So I guess your ambition is to grace the centrefold of some girlie mag, or one of the trashier newspapers. Well, who am I to disappoint you, especially when you've gone to such trouble.'

Before Somer could voice any protest he pinned her back on the towel, imprisoning her there with his superior weight, silencing her with the harsh pressure of his mouth, kissing her until red and black whorls flashed fierily behind the closed eyelids, her breasts peaking shamefully under the expert ministrations of his hands, her body so deeply awash with pleasure that it took several seconds for her to assimilate what was happening when he suddenly thrust her away from him and got up, striding over to where he had left his equipment.

'*Now* I'll photograph you,' he said harshly, 'now, while your body still bears all the signs of my lovemaking. The girlie mags will leap at the photographs I'm going to take, and when their customers look at you they'll be able to imagine *they're* making love to you; that *they're* the ones to bring that blind look of passion to your eyes and the tormenting fullness to your breasts. That's what you wanted, isn't it?' he demanded savagely, moving round her all the time he was speaking, his fury lashing down on her, keeping her motionless with dread on her towel, unable to do more than whimper a protest as the camera flashed. 'And again...' Chase taunted. 'Look at me this time. No, not like that.' He came over to her, watching her flinch away with cold anger as he bent towards her, his thumb rubbing provocatively across her bottom lip until she was shivering with the response she could not conceal. 'That's better.' The camera flashed again.

'No, please, you don't understand.' Somer was mortified. How could he think she wanted him to photograph her like this? It had just been a ploy to distract him, to buy time for herself while she plucked up the courage to go through with her plan, but it had all gone dreadfully wrong. She had never expected him to get up and leave her. She had wanted him to soothe and comfort her body into relaxed acceptance of his lovemaking, she admitted achingly, but instead...

'Please, Chase, you don't understand.'

He flung his equipment to one side, replacing his camera in its case, his face almost black with anger as he turned and came back to her. 'I understand all I need to. You invited yourself here today so that we could make love; so that you could get your photographs. Well, you've got them, now it's time to pay for them,' he told her crudely. 'Not so very long ago you were inviting me to make love to you, and by Hell I'm going to. There's just enough adrenalin pumping round my body now for anger and contempt to be an adequate substitute for the...the need I had of you before, and my hormones are still so crazily responsive to you that...'

'But you're so angry with me, you can't...' still want

me, Somer had been about to say, but she realised before the words left her lips that they were hopelessly naïve.

'Oh I think you'll find that I can, and adequately enough for you not to be too disappointed,' Chase assured her unpleasantly.

He came down beside her, gathering up the small fists she beat impotently against his chest, laughing deep in his throat, a sound which turned to a growl as he imprisoned her wrists, fastening her arms above her head.

Trembling with rage and humiliation Somer refused to give in to the urge to close her eyes, to blot out his bitterly triumphant smile and the green glitter in his eyes as his glance moved slowly down over her unprotected body. She could see her heart thumping beneath her ribs, hate quivering through her as Chase looked his lazy fill.

'My payment for doing what you wanted,' he said smoothly at last, 'and don't bother pretending you haven't used your body like this before. Your timing was too good for that. Wait until the poor guy's so wound up that he'll agree to anything to have you, is that it, Somer? Wait for the right psychological moment and you can get him to promise you the earth? Well, you made some promises of your own, and I'm going to see that you keep them, but I'm sure you'll understand and forgive me on this occasion if I simply take what you owe me without indulging in any further bargaining.'

He lowered himself easily on to her body, one hard knee defying all the attempts of her slim thighs and locked muscles to deny it access.

The hard muscled weight of him deprived her of breath, and Somer struggled to subdue her intense panic, reminding herself that this was what she had wanted. Chase had removed his swimming shorts and the feel of his naked body against her set off a fresh rush of alarm.

She felt Chase move against her, his hand on her hip before it slid between their bodies. The intimate brush of his fingers against her was something she hadn't been prepared for and she jumped, tensing her entire body, her eyes flying open as her body repelled his invading touch.

Fierce waves of trembling heat washed across her body, sending contradictory signals to her brain. Chase realigned his weight, leaning on his side, watching her closely as his hand returned to her hip, his thumb stroking her tense muscles. A shivering sigh of relief escaped her lips, quickly giving way to fresh panic as Chase moved again, releasing her captive wrists, guiding her hand down his body with an unmistakable purpose that tensed Somer's muscles and made her fingers curl protestingly into her palm. Her hand felt as cold as ice when Chase placed it on his thigh, her eyes sliding frantically away from his, panic and fear exploding inside her, as she struggled to subdue all her natural modesty and remember why she was here.

It was bad enough when she had thought Chase simply intended to almost rape her, but now, knowing he wanted and expected her to touch him as intimately as he had touched her, turned her brain into a tight ball of panic, every instinct urging flight.

'*You* want the photographs,' Chase murmured softly in her ear. 'You make love to me, Somer. It turns me on when the woman becomes the aggressor. Take me inside you, Somer, show me just how very good you are.'

Numb with panic Somer could only stare blindly up at him, her strangled, 'No, please...I can't,' so low that she was amazed that he heard it. 'I don't want the photographs,' she added wildly, 'I never wanted them, I...'

'Then what *did* you want?'

He moved so swiftly that she had no opportunity to

defend herself from the probing question. 'Well, Somer, what did you want?'

'I wanted you to make love to me.' She had no thought of lying. She felt too battered emotionally to think of even a half-way believable untruth.

'You did?' Dark eyebrows rose in sardonic disbelief. 'Well you have a funny way of showing it.'

'I wanted you to make love to me because I'm still a virgin,' Somer admitted wretchedly, too disheartened and miserable to keep the truth back any longer. She couldn't look at him, couldn't bear to see the expression on his face and so she rolled away from him, keeping her back to him, her voice muffled. 'I never wanted any photographs, I just…'

'Lost your nerve,' Chase said with heavy irony. 'I suppose I ought to have guessed. All the signs were there.'

Her face buried in her arms, Somer flushed dark red with humiliation. 'Oh yes, I know how useless I am as a sexual partner; what a turn-off I can be. I know I don't know how to please a man, how to…' Her voice rose with each sobbed admission. She had come so far, humiliated herself so much already. Chase had shown that physically he wasn't completely indifferent to her. She rolled over to face him, her eyes dark-bruised pansy violet in her small face. Inside she was a tightly clenched bundle of nerves, please let him say yes, she prayed earnestly, please, please. She took a deep breath and forced herself to meet the enigmatic blankness of his eyes.

'Chase, please, please would you make love to me?'

She couldn't endure the tense silence that followed her husky question.

'Somer.' She felt the warmth of his breath against her temple as he leaned towards her, his fingers splaying across her back. 'Somer, now isn't the time; try to understand…'

Oh she understood all right, he was rejecting her, just as Andrew had rejected her. He had wanted her when he thought she was experienced; but now he knew the truth he no longer felt any desire for her.

'I can't believe you simply woke up this morning and decided you wanted to lose your virginity, and to me,' she heard Chase saying calmly. 'We need to talk about this.'

'What is there to talk about?' Somer recognised the faint hysteria edging up under her voice. 'You don't want me. No one wants me. Andrew was right, I just don't have what it takes…'

'Andrew?' Chase demanded sharply.

'Yes, Andrew, the man I was engaged to until this morning, until I found him in bed with someone else, someone with the experience to give him what I can't. Someone who turns him on in a way that I'll never be able to. He's like you, you see,' she said evenly, wondering how her voice managed to seem so calm when she was being devoured, dying from the pain exploding inside her. 'He doesn't like virgins…'

'And it was because of him that you attached yourself to me this morning.' There was a look of grim incredulity about Chase's face that should have warned her of impending danger. 'You were going to let me make love to you…you wanted me to make love to you because of this Andrew? Somer, don't you know the dangers of acting like that? I came damn near raping you earlier on this afternoon, do you realise that? You deliberately let me think you were experienced, and not just experienced, but sexually casual as well. I could even have got you pregnant.'

His harsh words, plus the shock of his rejection had a sobering effect on her; shivering with shame and reaction

Somer acknowledged the truth of his words. The plain fact of the matter was that she had made herself a vow in the heat of temper which she could never have carried out once that temper had cooled; as it had been cooling before lunch, until she had consumed the three glasses of wine which had given her the Dutch courage to carry on, but over and above her acknowledgement of the truth of Chase's comments was a bitter feeling of rejection, worse in many ways than Andrew's had been. Chase didn't want her; he wasn't going to make love to her and she was going to be left with this curious ache deep down inside her that was tormenting her whole body.

'Look, we've got to talk about this. We'll go back to the hotel, and then we'll meet for dinner.'

'No,' Somer protested sharply, 'I never want to see you again, don't you understand?'

'Oh I understand all right, probably far better than you do,' Chase said grimly. 'I understand that you were going to use me; that you don't give a damn about me as a person, that you only wanted my body.' His mouth was a thin sneering line. 'Rather a role reversal, isn't it, and one I don't particularly like. Why, might I ask, did you pick me?'

'Because you looked experienced...and worldly,' Somer admitted.

'You never felt the slightest desire for *me* as a person then?' Chase questioned, something tight and tense about his body as he waited for her reply.

Somer shook her head. How could she have done when she loved Andrew?

'Get dressed, we're going back to the hotel.' He turned his back on her while he dressed, quickly and angrily, his shoulders tense. Shivering Somer pulled on her own clothes. Never in her life had she experienced such hu-

miliation; worse even than Andrew's rejection. When
Chase turned and accidently brushed her skin she froze,
her eyes dilating. He followed the movement, his mouth
twisting mockingly. 'How on earth did you think you were
going to endure my lovemaking when you flinch away
from me like that?'

'I just wanted to get it over with,' Somer muttered. 'I...'

'You were using me,' Chase ground out, grasping her
wrist and swinging her round. He was angry, bitterly angry
and she couldn't understand why. She was the one who
had been humiliated; rejected, tossed aside the moment he
knew the truth. 'Experimenting like the crazy adolescent
you still are.' He released her and bent to stuff his towel
into his bag, methodically packing away his camera equipment before setting out for the cliff path without another
word to Somer.

They drove back to the hotel in silence. Judith was on
reception when they walked in, and pride made Somer lift
her head and stare coolly at the other girl, unaware of how
fragile and graceful she looked walking at Chase's side,
her skin warmed by the sun, her lips still swollen from his
kisses.

'It's four o'clock now,' Chase told her, glancing at his
watch. 'I'll meet you down here at eight.' When she
opened her mouth to protest he said curtly, 'If you aren't
here I'll come to your room and drag you out. Tonight I
want the full story. Dear God, your father must be crazy
to let you loose on your own. Perhaps someone ought to
have a word with them.'

Somer shrank back. 'You wouldn't?'

'Wouldn't I? You'd be surprised how easy I'd find it.
Eight o'clock,' he told her curtly as he pushed her towards
the lift. 'And remember, if you aren't there I'll come looking for you.'

Once she had gained the sanctuary of her room, Somer stripped off her clothes and stepped into the shower. Her skin was faintly bruised where Chase had gripped her, her breasts fuller than usual. As she soaped her skin she couldn't help remembering how she had felt when Chase had kissed her nipples. Unbidden the mental image of his dark head nestled against her pale skin rose up to taunt her, but she banished it reminding herself bitterly that his passion had soon died once he knew the truth. Just like Andrew, he hadn't wanted her; he had rejected her.

Pain was a great tearing anguish inside her chest. She wanted to cry and scream but the emotions were all locked up inside her. Never, ever again would anyone get the opportunity to reject her as Chase had rejected her today, even if that meant she had to stay a virgin for the rest of her life. At least that way she got to keep her pride and self-respect. Judith and Andrew had been right; he hadn't wanted her. No man would want her once they knew the truth, and that being the case it was better that they never got the opportunity to find out. As for meeting Chase for dinner—she remembered his threat about her father and shuddered. How disappointed in her her father would be if he ever learned what Chase had to say. How glad she was now that she had only told him her Christian name. Wrapping her body in a thick warm towel she made her way to the telephone, dialling reception.

Fortunately it wasn't Judith who answered but one of the other girls, who listened while Somer explained what she wanted, and then asked her to hold.

One minute, two, three…impatiently, her stomach tense with nerves Somer counted the seconds.

'Yes, that's fine, Miss MacDonald,' the girl said at last. 'There's a seat on tonight's flight. It leaves at six thirty, so that doesn't leave you much time. I'll order a taxi for you, if you let us know when you're packed.'

Thanking her for her help Somer replaced the receiver with a feeling of relief. By six thirty. That meant that at eight o'clock while Chase Lorimer was waiting for her in the foyer, she would be safely back home in Aberdeen. She went white and then red as she pictured Chase returning to London, laughing about her to his friends, describing in intimate detail what had happened between them, mocking her innocence and inexperience; and they would laugh, all those glamorous people he no doubt knew.

Swift pain pierced through her mingling with it a melancholic sadness; an aching sense of irretrievable loss; a sensation that her life had changed and would never be the same again, a confirmation of all those inner warnings she had ignored, telling her not to get involved with Chase Lorimer.

Half a day spent together was hardly an involvement, she told herself wryly, not wanting to admit the kind of involvement there would always be between a man and a woman whose bodies had known one another intimately. Only they hadn't. Chase had rejected her.

ALTHOUGH SHE didn't know it then by the time she stepped out of the plane at Aberdeen she had made the painful transition from adolescence to adulthood. Adulthood, but never womanhood; womanhood had been denied her by a man with dark hair and green eyes, a man who had taught her body to feel desire and then had cruelly robbed it of satisfaction. A man whom she would never forget and who would haunt her for as long as she lived.

It never once struck Somer as odd as she settled back in the cab carrying her home that it was Chase Lorimer on whom her thoughts centred and not Andrew to whom she had been engaged. Chase Lorimer's crime was the greater. Andrew loved someone else; his rejection was in some part understandable, he had never truly desired her, only her father's wealth, but Chase had wanted her; had told her so both in actions and words—until she told him she was a virgin. And it was then when she had humbled herself to ask for his help and understanding that he had rejected her; refused her; and that was something she could never forget.

CHAPTER FOUR

'Looks good, doesn't it?' Somer teased her father, leaning over his shoulder to study the announcement in the paper. 'Sir Duncan MacDonald, British Ambassador to Qu'Hoor.'

'It isn't official yet,' Sir Duncan warned her, closing the paper and putting it on one side as he kissed her cheek. The last five years had brought many changes, not least those in his daughter. One minute, or so it seemed to him in retrospect, she had been a child, lovable, very pretty but still a child, the next she was a woman, awesome, faintly mysterious. He sighed as she slipped into the chair opposite him and began her breakfast. He had noticed the change when she came back from Jersey, her engagement broken. He had asked her if she wanted to talk about it but she had refused. It was over, she had said, and that was all there was to say. He couldn't pretend that he hadn't been relieved, he had never been happy about the engagement. How deeply had its ending hurt her? Not very deeply, he would have said five years ago when it happened, but now...

Three years ago Sefton Oil had opened new headquarters in London and as Chairman Sir Duncan had moved with them. So had Somer, taking up the reins of managing his new London establishment so easily and graciously that he had heaved a sigh of relief and turned his attentions to strengthening the position of the company. His sound judgement and innate business flair had been well repaid.

Sefton Oil was an extremely successful company, so successful that Sir Duncan had felt few qualms about leaving its future in the hands of the capable directors he had hand-picked for their jobs. And now new horizons beckoned. It had been the Prime Minister's idea to appoint an ambassador to the potentially troublesome Middle Eastern state, not from the ranks of the Foreign Office but from industry, and the choice had fallen on Sir Duncan. Somehow the news had been leaked to the press although his appointment was not yet official and several of the morning's newspapers carried articles about him on their financial and gossip column pages, one or two including photographs of Somer, who was to act as his hostess at the Embassy.

Surely one of the reasons Sir Duncan had been chosen, one of the more well informed papers opined, was because of his unblemished career record; his reputation for honesty, loyalty and tolerance; the good manners and negotiating skill for which he was famous. Somer MacDonald, like her father, possessed an unimpeachable character, important when taking into account the delicate nature of her father's mission; Qu'Hoor was well documented as being a rigidly Muslim country; women were expected to abide by a code of morals long since out of fashion in the West, and for the new Ambassador's daughter and hostess to be recognised as a typically Western woman used to indulging in affairs and liaisons whenever the mood struck her would reflect adversely on Sir Duncan, causing him to lose 'face' in his host country.

All this had been explained to Sir Duncan when he was initially interviewed for the post, and he in turn had told Somer. There was a good deal of Foreign Office opposition to his proposed appointment, and he had added frankly that he was relieved that in this instance at least he knew he need have no fears or concerns. 'I know it's unfair,' he had agreed when Somer had raised a mocking eyebrow. 'Muslim men certainly don't abide by the same code they impose on their women, but that's the way it is. If you'd rather not come with me...'

'It isn't that, and even if I didn't would it make any difference if it was widely known that my character wasn't as pure as the driven snow?'

'It certainly would. Even if you decided not to come with me, I doubt if I'd be selected if there was anything about my personal history which would mean me forfeiting the Qu'Hoorian Government's respect.'

'As serious as that?'

When he had confirmed it, Somer had fallen silent, thinking ironically about the past. It was five years since that awful time on Jersey, five years since she had sworn to herself that never again would any man get the opportunity to reject her, and she had stuck rigidly to that vow. Anyone who dated her and who tried to cross the invisible boundaries she set around herself quickly found himself excluded from her circle of dates. She made it a rule never to date any man more than twice in one month, and she knew quite well that she had the reputation of being cold and unattainable. Not that that prevented certain diehards from trying. There was always the lure of her father's wealth, she thought wryly, picking up his paper and studying the article it was running on him yet again.

Did she really want to leave Britain? She had acted as her father's hostess for five years now, and while she enjoyed the task, it had ceased to be absorbing not long after they moved to London. Physically busy but mentally bored she had enrolled on a course on computer technology, and now was greatly in demand writing computer programmes for various companies. In addition to providing her with mental stimulation, it also brought her in a quite substantial income—certainly sufficient to live independently from her father if she wished. Her father wasn't pressing her to go to Qu'Hoor. Because it was a strict Muslim country she would be remaining strictly in the background of his life, 'unless some sheikh offers me half a dozen oil wells for you,' he had teased her several days ago.

'I think he'll find he's bought a pig in a poke if he does,' had been her dry response. The male sex held no attraction for her. It was as though her emotions had frozen that day on the beach with Chase Lorimer and they had remained in that deep-frozen state every since. Oh, she was not as naïve as she had been then; she had shared kisses, quite pleasurably, with her dates, wondering with fine irony if her lips left them as cold as theirs left her, and then assuming that they probably did when they made no attempts to take their lovemaking any further. But then she had perfected the art of repelling their advances almost before they were made. She cultivated a cool remote air that could sometimes have the effect of wiping the smile entirely from a man's eyes; a subtle trick of looking at them as though she somehow found them wanting; rejecting them before they ever got the chance to reject her.

Only she knew of those long-drawn-out hours of the night when she lay awake brought face to face with her own deep insecurities, the knowledge that her make-up lacked some elemental component. She was a woman in every sense but the truest one. A cold, aloof, animated statue was how one of her dates had disgustedly described her, and she knew it was true. She had no inner warmth or fire with which to attract or hold a man, and rather than submit to the degradation of one of them discovering the truth, she preferred to hold herself completely aloof. Like some Cinderella awaiting the magic kiss which could free her from her body's icy indifference, she mocked herself as she folded her father's paper and excused herself from the table. She was half-way through a particularly complicated programme, and wanted to get it finished.

The room she worked in was furnished in soft feminine colours and fabrics, soft yellow walls; a settee covered in an attractive yellow and blue print, and a toning blue carpet. The bank of computer equipment she used to work on was in a small room off her study, and as she made her way there she stopped to pick up the receiver of the ringing telephone.

'Stan Fellows here from the *Globe*, Miss MacDonald,' she heard a male voice announce. 'How do you feel about going to Qu'Hoor?'

The *Globe* reporter wasn't the first to ring her after the leaked announcement of her father's appointment, and for his sake Somer had made a point of dealing with their questions in a pleasant but non-committal manner. She explained politely that as it was not yet official that her father had the appointment, she was not able to make any formal comment.

'Not even when I tell you that Clinton Towers has been quoted as saying that a spell in the desert might help you thaw out a bit?'

Mentally seething Somer forced herself not to retaliate. Clinton Towers had been in line for a directorship with Sefton Oil several months ago, and had tried to consolidate his position by dating Somer. She hadn't been at all deceived. It had happened too often before and the fine intelligence she had had at eighteen had been honed over the years almost to the point of a sixth sense which told her when she was being used.

When she had heard that Clinton Towers was boasting that Sir Duncan would soon be his father-in-law, Somer had felt obliged to take action. Unfortunately Clinton had been unwise enough to make his boast in the hearing of another journalist who had lost no time in publishing it, followed a matter of days later by the gleeful revelation that far from being on the point of announcing her engagement, Somer MacDonald had been overheard to say that one oilman in the family was enough and that she had no intention of marrying another. Clinton had come storming round to see her, and during the ensuing row had left her in no doubt at all just what he had found attractive about her. She hadn't seen Clinton since and had presumed that their final scene was the end of the matter. Now she realised she had been wrong. There was nothing quite so vindictive as a small-minded, spurned male, she decided, fingers curling tightly round the receiver as she fought for control, finally saying smoothly, 'Mr Towers's views are his own and he is perfectly free to voice them if he so chooses.'

Realising that he was not going to get anything out of her the journalist hung up. Sighing Somer walked through to her equipment. She would be glad when her father's appointment was made official. She hadn't realised how much strain would be involved in keeping the press at bay until it was. The problem was that the appointment was a very sensitive issue, partly because of Qu'Hoor itself and partly because of Foreign Office disapproval. They would be waiting to leap on any slip, or *faux pas* her father made; any small morsel of gossip which might back up their claim that he was not the right choice.

Grimly she started to work, but she could not concentrate. Pushing aside her work she wandered back into her study and poured herself a cup of coffee from the bubbling percolator. Her father's secretary had brought her mail in and she flicked through it in a desultory fashion, slitting the envelopes methodically and removing the contents.

Most of her correspondence related to work she had on hand, or queries as to whether she intended to continue with her work if she left the country. There was also a bank statement showing a pleasantly healthy balance, a postcard from a friend on holiday in the Seychelles, and finally the last letter. Spiky, imperious writing slashed across the envelope, and she frowned, not recognising it, yet wondering why she should feel this faint prickling of alarm.

Almost reluctantly she removed the notepaper from inside, noting that it was thick and expensive. As she smoothed out the single sheet her eyes dropped automatically to the signature at the bottom. It was like receiving a stunning blow in the chest. Her breath strangled in her throat, her heart seizing up between heartbeats as she studied the heavy black script disbelievingly. Chase Lorimer, what on earth was he writing to her for?

At first she had winced every time she saw his name in print, feeling almost sick with shame and humiliation, but gradually she had learned to cope with the almost violent emotions the sight of his name aroused. Two years ago there had been an announcement in the press to the effect that he was leaving the world of fashion photography and taking up a directorship with a newly formed television company. Not that it had seemed to make much difference, she thought, dry-mouthed. He still seemed to be photographed just as much, always with a beautiful female companion hanging adoringly on his arm. But why had he written to her?

She read his note quickly, and then again with stunned disbelief. He wanted to see her? But why? Why now, after all this time? When she first left Jersey she had started up

every time the phone or doorbell rang, dreading hearing
from him in case he revealed her foolish behaviour to her
father, but gradually as time went by she had ceased to
fear. So why did she feel something that was close to terror
icing through her veins now? Why had he got in touch
with her? Had he seen her photograph in the papers and
recognised her? It was a possibility but it didn't explain
his curt note, asking…no, commanding, she corrected herself wryly, that she call on him at his flat. 'Six o'clock
sharp on the 23rd', it stated, but it was not that that brought
the searing dread rushing over her, it was the brief para-
graph that followed. 'If you can't make the appointment,
I shall call on you at your home.' Innocuous enough
words, so why did she have the unshakeable feeling that
they contained a subtle threat? Shivering she glanced at
her calendar. Today was the 23rd. It was tonight that he
wanted to see her. She had two options open to her. She
could simply not go, which was what she wanted to do,
but if she took that course, she ran the risk of him appearing at the house, perhaps bumping into her father who
would naturally be curious. She had never once mentioned
Chase Lorimer's name in connection with her visit to Jersey, and if Chase did so… She bit her lip, her mind turning
in panicky circles. She knew her father had not totally
accepted her explanation that her engagement with Andrew had been broken off by mutual consent because they
had both realised they had made a mistake, but the whole
episode had been far too painful for her to discuss with
anyone and he had acceded to her plea that they simply
did not talk about it.

And she knew it would be foolhardy to place any reli-
ance on Chase Lorimer simply making an idle threat when
he said he would come to the house. Even at eighteen she
had had some intelligence, and what she remembered of

him told her that he was a man who meant exactly what he said.

A knock on her door startled her, her apprehension showing when she opened it. Her father's housekeeper stood outside, a tray holding Somer's lunch in her hand.

'My goodness,' she exclaimed with a smile, 'you are looking fierce. Is something wrong?'

Mrs McLeod had been with them in Aberdeen and had moved with them to London. She was the nearest thing to an older female confidante that Somer had ever had, and she grimaced slightly, glancing into a mirror, stunned by the wild glitter in her eyes, and the hectic rose colour warming her normally pale skin. Even her hair seemed to have reacted to Chase Lorimer's cryptic note, adding to her tempestuous appearance.

'Nothing at all, just a sudden bout of temper,' she told the housekeeper ruefully, watching the grey eyebrows rise. Somer wasn't given to bouts of temper, sudden or otherwise, and Sarah McLeod's mobilely lifted eyebrows expressed her disbelief. She liked Somer and being more intuitive than her father had instantly noticed the change in her after her engagement had been broken off, putting her own interpretation on Somer's sudden withdrawal inside the protective shell she had carried round with her ever since.

'Will you both be in for dinner?'

'Umm. Yes... That is, I have to go out later this afternoon but I shouldn't be gone very long.'

It wasn't until the words left her mouth that Somer realised she had made her decision. Once made it ought to have been easy for her to settle down and concentrate on her work—previously a never-failing means of blocking out things she would rather not think about—but on this occasion Chase Lorimer's sudden intrusion into her life was too powerful for her to blot out. She shuddered, images she would rather not remember crowding vividly into her mind. Had she really pleaded with him to make love to her? It seemed like a wildly impossible dream now—a nightmare more like, and, yes, it had been true, despite the fact that she would rather believe it had not. What was it about the man that gave him the power to affect her so profoundly that even Mrs McLeod had been aware of the change in her appearance?

She got up and prowled round her sitting-room like a nervous cat, refusing to find comfort in the softly pretty colours, glancing at herself in the mirror she used to check her appearance before meeting anyone. Her dark hair which she normally wore in a soft coil was loose, her eyes normally so cool, deeply violet, her mouth surely fuller and softer than normal. Five years had fined down her body revealing her elegant bone structure. Breasts which she privately thought too full were subtly disguised by the blouse she wore. High-necked and long-sleeved its pale amethyst colour matched her eyes, her straight cream skirt skimming the narrow bones of her hips and ending well below her knees. Quietly elegant was how her father described her choice of clothes. Once or twice he had urged her to try something a little more daring but she had always refused.

At four o'clock she went upstairs, rifling through her wardrobe, looking for something suitable to wear. In the end she chose a well-cut black suit and picked out a white blouse to wear with it, carefully brushing her hair into a smooth coil, and standing back to study the finished effect, inwardly congratulating herself when she saw her reflection.

Yes, the whole effect was very cool and remote. No one seeing her dressed like this could ever, ever mistake her for a tearful flushed eighteen-year-old, begging to be made love to.

'Going somewhere?' her father asked curiously when she bumped into him in the hallway. 'I didn't know you were out this evening.'

'Something cropped up,' Somer explained vaguely, knowing her father would assume that she was going out on business and not wanting to commit herself to a direct lie. 'But I should be back in time for dinner.'

'Umm, I'm not sure if I'm going to make it though. I got a call from the PM's secretary this afternoon—urgent meetings tonight. It seems the FO are still making protesting noises about my appointment. Tonight I'm going to talk to the Qu'Hoorian Ambassador Sheikh Najur Ben Zayad—he's an extremely strict Muslim and apparently a force to be reckoned with in Qu'Hoor.'

'Yes, his appointment's a fairly recent one, isn't it?' Somer asked him. 'I remember reading about it. Wasn't there some sort of fuss about one of his daughters?'

'She wanted to attend a western university. Apparently the Sheikh was working in America at the time, and there was some suggestion from him that he though the Americans had been influencing his daughter to rebel. She was at school there. I suspect tonight's meeting is going to be something of a personal vetting.' Sir Duncan frowned and Somer walked across to him, smiling lovingly.

'You really want this post, don't you?' she said softly.

'Does it show so much?' He sighed. 'I must admit I'd be terribly disappointed if I didn't get it now. I've gone as far as I can with Sefton Oil—it can function perfectly well without me now, and I enjoyed most the days when we were building it up. This ambassadorship will be a new challenge. Scots always enjoy travelling—we're nation builders in every sense of the word, and I suppose I'm idealistic enough to hope that I could do something to ensure unity between Britain and Qu'Hoor.'

It wasn't very far from her father's St John's Wood house to the address Chase Lorimer had given her; in fact the drive seemed alarmingly brief. Somer had elected to drive herself; the sporty Mercedes she had bought for herself out of her own earnings. The shiny scarlet car was her pride and joy, although she managed to conceal the fact under a coolly matter-of-fact exterior.

After consulting her A to Z she found the address without too much difficulty. Chase Lorimer lived not in a modern apartment block as she had imagined but in a gracious terrace of houses overlooking the river. Slowing down to a crawl she searched for a parking spot almost right outside. At exactly six o'clock she stepped out of her car and locked it, walking as calmly as she could up the brief flight of steps to the shiny black front door. A brass doorknocker in the shape of a gargoyle confronted her and lifting it decisively she rapped smartly on the door. The sound was dying away slowly when she heard sounds of movement inside. The door opened inwards and she hovered reluctantly on the doorstep, suddenly seized by alarm.

'Exactly on time,' a deep male voice that sent shivers of recognition down her spine drawled. 'Please come in. I wondered when I saw you sitting outside whether you were having second thoughts.'

It was distinctly unnerving to know that he had watched her sitting in her car; and had perhaps witnessed the vulnerability of her face when she had thought herself unobserved.

A brief touch on her arm sent tension coiling through her. 'Look, I haven't got much time, just tell me why you wanted to see me, will you?'

'Perhaps I wanted to see if the reality was as beautiful

as your photographs,' he said suavely, reaching above her head to push open a door. 'Surely you've got time to sit down and have a drink?'

She stiffened and glanced frostily into his relaxed face. Five years ago she had been struck by his sexuality, but her reaction then had been nothing compared to the assault on her senses his masculinity afforded now. She could feel the shock of it reverberating the length of her body, jolting down her tense spine. Nothing about him had changed. His eyes were still that same deep, dark jade, his skin tanned, his mouth curling with the sardonic amusement she remembered so vividly. His body was as lean and hard-muscled as ever, although the clothes were different, a well tailored suit and a crisp white shirt replacing the jeans and shirts she remembered. Studying him surreptitiously through her lashes, Somer felt her pulses thud out a warning. This man was dangerous; he had been dangerous five years ago and he was even more dangerous now.

As she watched, he shot back a snowy cuff and studied the gold watch strapped to his wrist calmly. 'It's now five minutes past six,' he informed her, 'and we've already wasted five minutes of your valuable time. Of course,' he continued smoothly, 'I appreciate your need to make an inventory…' Hot colour bloomed in her face. So he hadn't missed the fact that she was studying him. 'I've been making one of my own.' His eyes slid with deliberate purpose over her body, a smile twitching the corners of his mouth. 'Very effective,' he drawled. 'You look like an extremely cool, controlled lady.'

'Probably because I am,' Somer retorted, goaded by the mockery in his look, but getting a grip on her runaway temper almost immediately. 'Look, I don't know why you wanted to see me.'

'All in good time. First a drink…'

Somehow he was behind her, leaving her no alternative but to turn through the door into the elegantly furnished drawing-room. The cool blues and creams with the odd touch of rose to warm up the colour-scheme had been chosen with care and a subtle eye to colour. The furnishings were traditional and somehow surprising. If she had taken the time to consider the sort of background Chase Lorimer would choose, which she hadn't, she would have picked out a modern apartment, starkly furnished with modern eye-catching furniture, not this under-stated elegance; these rich colours and beautiful antiques.

'You look very at home sitting there,' he commented, as he walked over to a concealed cabinet and opened it.

'It hardly matters whether I look at home here or not,' Somer retorted icily. 'Will you please tell me what you want…?'

'Oh I think it does…' Chase mused, ignoring the second part of her speech. 'You see I want you to feel at home here, Somer, after all that's what this house is going to be—your home. At least when we're not living in the country. I have a house there too you know.'

'What…' Somer's mouth gaped, her mind racing in its frantic efforts to follow his conversation.

'I want you to marry me, Somer,' Chase continued lazily, pouring them both a drink—without asking her for her choice, Somer noted angrily.

'Marry you? Have you gone mad? I don't intend to marry anyone—least of all you.'

'Why least of all me? Because you once asked me to make love to you and I refused? Would it help if I told you I regretted making that mistake, but you had me somewhat off guard, you see, Somer…I had no idea.'

'I don't want to talk about the past,' Somer stormed

bitterly at him. 'And if this…this proposal of yours is your
idea of a joke?'

'No joke,' he told her, walking towards her and handing
her a crystal sherry-glass half full of pale amber liquid, his
face grimly composed as he sat down opposite her. 'Believe me it's no joke at all.'

'Well, you've made your proposal and I've refused and
now I'm going to leave,' Somer told him curtly, putting
her glass down on an elegant Edwardian sofa table and
standing up. 'You aren't the first man who's wanted to
marry the daughter of Sir Duncan MacDonald, and Sefton
Oil, and I don't expect you'll be the last, but at least the
others showed some finesse.'

'Like Clinton Towers did, do you mean?' Chase
drawled, not in the slightest bit disturbed by her angry
outburst. 'Well you needn't worry about that, I'm not the
least interested in Sefton Oil or the fact that you're Sir
Duncan MacDonald's daughter, or at least only in so far
as those facts work to my advantage.'

'One of those advantages being my father's wealth, I
suppose?' she asked with heavy irony. Somehow Chase
had interposed himself between her and the door, on which
he was now leaning with studied negligence but with a
look in his eyes which told her it would be extremely
foolhardy, not to say potentially humiliating for her to try
to force her way past.

'My, my, you do have a low self-image, don't you?
Well, I assure you that my reasons for wanting to marry
you have nothing to do with your father's wealth.'

'No?'

'No. As a matter of fact, I'm now an extremely wealthy
man myself, or at least I shall be once I comply with the
terms of my uncle's will.'

'Which are?' Why on earth had she asked him that?

What could it possibly matter to her what terms his uncle's will stipulated? All she wanted to do was to escape from his room and his far too overwhelming presence before she forgot that she wasn't eighteen any longer.

'That I must marry within three months of his death. You see my uncle was a great believer in family life.'

'And you're so hard up for a bride that you had to choose me?' Somer mocked.

'You're showing your low self-esteem again,' Chase retaliated. 'Why do you find it so impossible to believe I might have asked you simply because I want you?'

'The way you wanted me five years ago?' She couldn't keep the betraying pain out of her voice, and moved quickly and unsteadily, trying to recover her composure, reaching for her sherry and then setting the glass down again as it trembled in her fingers. 'This has gone far enough. I don't know what stupid game you think you're playing, Chase, but I really must leave now.'

He was still blocking her exit, arms folded across his chest, and her mind traitorously relayed to her a mental image of how that chest looked—and felt.

'No game, Somer,' Chase told her lightly. 'I intend to marry you.'

'Because after five years you've suddenly discovered you're madly in love with a woman you couldn't even bring yourself to make love to? I won't buy that, Chase,' she told him steadily.

'No, I don't suppose you would. Why did you run out on me that night, Somer?'

'Don't you think we'd said all there was to say to one another?' Her voice sounded light and precariously brittle.

'You mean I wouldn't oblige so you went out and found someone else who would?' His tone was deceptively soft, smokily dangerous, each clear-cut word reverberating in her ears.

'And if I did?' Pride made her lift her head and confront him with eyes amethyst with mingled anger and pain.

'You pretty soon discovered that sex for sex's sake can be a very soul-destroying business—at least if all that one hears and reads about you is correct. The press seem to be giving you a lot of space these days—since your father has been chosen to represent the country abroad. In fact it seems to me that his daughter's unimpeachable moral standards are working very much in Sir Duncan's favour at the moment.'

'And?' Somer questioned sensing that the trap was closing round her and yet not knowing why she should feel so keenly aware of encroaching danger.

'And, if you don't agree to marry me, I might, just might be forced to reveal to the press exactly how much they've underestimated you. I'm sure they'll believe me, especially when they see my photographs.'

Somer went pale, grasping the edge of the settee and forcing back the nauseous faintness clamouring inside her.

'That's blackmail,' she whispered drily, hardly able to credit what she was hearing, her revulsion plainly revealed in her voice.

'Some might call it that, I merely consider it good gamesmanship. I want you for my wife, Somer, and I'm prepared to use every advantage I have at my disposal to make sure you marry me.'

'But why?'

'Why?' His mouth curled sardonically. 'The eternal cry of a too-intelligent woman. There are others of your sex, my dear, who would simply accept my words at face value, who would find it quite easy to accept that I wanted them for themselves alone, but you aren't able to delude yourself as easily, are you?'

It hurt, just as he had meant it to, but she straightened her spine and faced him bravely. 'How could I? You made it plain how you felt about me five years ago, Chase. You didn't want me then, why should you want me now?'

'Because you, my dear, are the only woman I know who will consent to marry me on my terms. That is to say, in twelve months' time when my uncle's will has been satisfactorily proved and I have inherited, you will be quite happy to bow out of my life, because I have the means to ensure that you do so.'

'The photographs.' Her eyes almost black with pain, Somer whispered the words through a painfully dry throat.

'The photographs,' Chase agreed. 'Here they are.' He opened his jacket and removed a package from one pocket. 'Of course these are on the small side, but I've kept the negatives—however, I'm sure once you see these you'll…'

Somer wasn't listening. She was staring at the envelope he had tossed to her as though it were a live snake.

'Aren't you going to look at them? I could be bluffing, after all.'

'I don't want to see them.' How tight and strained her voice sounded. She felt as though an iron band had tightened round her throat, every syllable uttered was a tearing pain.

'Oh, I think you should.' With one fluid movement Chase detached himself from the door and came towards her. The door was now left unbarred but she felt no urge to flee. With sick fascination she watched him flip open the manilla envelope and extract half a dozen glossy prints. The colours blurred and danced before her anguished eyes, her face losing every vestige of colour.

'No...' Her denial was a long-drawn-out, tormented protest, her eyes closing, her fingers curling into tense fists of protest.

'Yes,' Chase's voice was implacably smooth. She felt the settee depress beneath his weight; and even through her closed eyelids she was aware of the male heat emanating from him. His determination was an almost palpable thing in the pleasant room, reaching out to enfold and impale her. Cool fingers grasped her own, a mocking voice close to her ear whispering, 'But why such reluctance? I seem to remember you were the one who wanted me to take them.'

'Because I was frightened.' The admission burst past her trembling lips. 'Because I was fighting to buy time...I couldn't think of any other way to...'

'To stop me making love to you? And yet not ten minutes later you were begging me to do so. I wonder if you have any idea of how I felt when I came downstairs that evening and found you gone? Knowing the state you were in I went half out of my mind worrying about you. No one seemed to know a damned thing about you. Not your address...I even checked the register myself, but all there was was your name.'

'Very touching.' Her cold words silenced him. 'But I don't believe a word you're saying. If you were so concerned about me why are you blackmailing me like this now?'

'I've told you. I need a wife to conform with the terms of my uncle's will. Marriage—a permanent marriage that is—isn't part of my plans right now, and neither do I much care for the thought of paying out a substantial sum of money to rid myself of a wife I never wanted in the first place. With modern divorce laws what they are I could well lose at least half of what I'll inherit. The house my uncle left me costs one hell of a lot to keep up—far more than I could afford on my present salary. If I had to pay over a substantial part of my income to an ex-wife, I could never afford to keep it.'

'So you hit on the ingenious idea of blackmailing me to marry you knowing you could divorce me the moment it suited you by holding the threat of exposing those photographs over me?' Her mouth curled disdainfully. 'I'm surprised you're not trying to blackmail me financially as well.'

Mockery gleamed in the green eyes slanted in her direction. 'I doubt that most men wouldn't be content with just you, Somer, especially if they could see you as I've seen you.'

'You're despicable.' The husky words whispered past her taut throat. 'I can't believe you really mean this.'

'Believe it.' The comment was laconically brief. 'I mean to collect my inheritance. Barnwell Manor was the only real home I knew as a child—my father was in the army and we—my mother, my sister and I—travelled around the world with him. Both he and my mother were killed by a bomb in Cyprus when I was nine—I was at boarding-school at the time. My uncle practically brought us up, but like I say he had strong views about the benefits of marriage. He never married himself and towards the end of his life he regretted it.'

'You don't have the slightest compunction about cheating him? About claiming your inheritance under false pretences?'

'No one dictates to me the terms on which I live my life, Somer.' His voice hardened imperceptibly. 'However, who knows, perhaps I'll enjoy being married to you so much that you'll make a convert out of me.'

'What makes you think I'll want to? I have no intention of marrying you or anyone else...'

'Because you don't want to limit yourself to one man?' His voice was smooth, but there was something dangerous and predatory glittering in his eyes that made her mouth go dry and her pulses race nervously. 'But you don't have the choice, not unless you want to see your father lose the ambassadorship, which he will do if these prints of you are published.'

Somer knew he spoke the truth. She glanced down to avoid his too-penetrating gaze, her eyes falling to the prints. One in particular shimmered in front of her and she stared at it, unable to drag her gaze away, her heart pounding with fear, her whole body reacting to the sight of her own nudity; to the slumberous, sexually aroused expression in her eyes. Her features were instantly recognisable to anyone able to drag their eyes off her nude body long enough to look at her face, but bad as the nudity of her body was, it was the expression in her eyes, so mercilessly caught by the cruel eye of the camera that betrayed her the most. I want to be made love to, those eyes said, and no one looking at the photograph could doubt how that photographic session had ended. No one apart from Chase and herself, that was.

'I must have time to think,' she said huskily, forcing herself to look up at him. 'I...'

'You've got twenty-four hours. If you haven't given me your answer then, within another twenty-four these prints will be in the hands of the press.'

'Please...' The word trembled on her lips and unbidden the memory of her pleading with this man once before rose up to torment her. She stood up shakily, noticing that this time he didn't bar her way to the door.

'Twenty-four hours, Somer,' he reminded her as he

opened the front door for her, 'and this time don't try running away.'

How could she when there was nowhere to run to, Somer asked herself half hysterically as she drove home. She had been gone less than two hours, but those two hours had drastically altered the course of her life. With every thread of common sense and logic she possessed she wanted to refuse Chase Lorimer's proposal, but if she did he would carry out his threat and her father would lose the post he wanted so badly.

She could hardly touch her dinner, and in order to assuage her father's anxious comments she lied that she had a headache. 'I thought you weren't dining at home tonight,' she commented, remembering his appointment with the Prime Minister.

'The meeting was over sooner than I anticipated. I must say I feel quite relieved. The Sheikh was very pleasant,' he grinned down the length of the mahogany table at his daughter, 'he even went as far as to say that you might be a good influence on his daughter. In fact I think it was the press reports of your sturdy moral fibre that finally won him over. Somer, are you sure you're all right?' The brief sound of pain his daughter made, and the glass of wine cascading over the table brought him to his feet.

'It's just this awful headache,' Somer lied. 'I'll be fine. I think I'll go to my room and lie down for a while. I'll probably have an early night.'

Once in her room she made no attempt to prepare for bed. If she did she knew she would not sleep. Round and round in exhausting circles her thoughts chased one another, searching frantically for some means of escape but knowing that there was none. How could she let her father down, but if she didn't she would be committed to twelve months of marriage to Chase Lorimer—twelve months living with a man she feared and loathed; the only man who knew the real truth about her; who knew how ineffective she was as a woman. Did you find someone else, he had asked her, and she hadn't denied it. Neither would she ever let him discover the truth. She couldn't endure the humiliation of his knowing that she was still a virgin; that she had never found anyone to relieve her of her unwanted innocence.

Morning found her pale-faced and heavy-eyed, her decision made. Had she ever had any real choice, she asked herself bitterly as she composed a brief note to Chase Lorimer. No doubt he wouldn't be surprised by her acquiescence. He had known all along that she would have to give in. Their marriage would be in name only, she had written—that way at least she was the one doing the rejecting this time. No doubt he hadn't intended anything different, she was making the point that this time she desired anything physical between them as little as he did.

She delivered the note herself, dashing back to her car the moment she had slipped it through his letter box. She had given him the answer he wanted, the next step was up to him. What form would it take? And how was she going to break the news to her father?

He had been in jubilant mood over breakfast, suggesting that they have a celebratory meal that evening. 'I'll give Peter Ferris a ring and ask him and Moira to join us, shall I?'

Peter Ferris was the Chief Executive of Sefton Oil and Somer's godfather. She had nodded her head numbly, promising to make all the arrangements with Mrs McLeod.

'And wear something really ravishing,' Sir Duncan had suggested, 'it might be your last opportunity—it's going to be strictly purdah once we arrive in Qu'Hoor.'

Somer dressed for her father's dinner party with scant

enthusiasm. The dress she had chosen matched her mood. It was black velvet with a demure boat-shaped neckline at the front, plunging almost to the waist at the back, tight sleeves hugging her arms, the skirt belling out softly from a fitted waist. Her father had chosen the dress and privately Somer knew it would never have been her choice. Despite its apparent demureness, the contrast of the black velvet to the delicately pale skin of her exposed back projected an image she wasn't entirely happy with. She would never have chosen to wear it at a larger gathering, but Peter Ferris was a close and old friend of her father's, close to his age, and he treated Somer much as though she were his daughter.

Coiling her hair at the back of her head she snapped on diamond-drop earrings, closing a matched diamond-studded bangle round her wrist.

'My word, you certainly took my advice to heart,' Sir Duncan applauded when Somer came downstairs. 'That's the dress I bought you for your birthday, isn't it?' He sounded so delighted that she was wearing it that Somer felt a pang of guilt. Her father was hardly likely to realise that she normally avoided wearing it because she knew it was basically a very seductive dress, projecting an image she felt it was impossible for her to live up to.

The doorbell chimed as they stood in the hall and Sir Duncan frowned, glancing at his watch. 'They're early, it's barely gone seven.' He strode forward to open the door, and Somer standing behind him felt the blood drain out of her face as she saw Chase Lorimer walk in.

'Good evening, sir,' he said easily. 'Now darling, no protests, I know you didn't want me to do this, but I'm damned if I'm going to part with you for six weeks, never mind six months.'

Somer's mouth had fallen open during this mocking recital, her face burning with hectic colour as she felt her father turn to her, confusion very evident in his expression.

'Somer...' he began, but Chase Lorimer didn't let him get any further.

'Somer has promised to marry me, Sir Duncan,' he said smoothly, 'I know she hasn't spoken to you about it. We'd just made up our minds when you discovered that you might get the post in Qu'Hoor. I agreed that we would delay our engagement for six months—she felt that she had to go with you at least for the first few months, but I know you'll understand when I tell you how reluctant I am to let her out of my sight for one month, never mind six. I want to marry her, Sir Duncan, and I want to marry her now, before you leave for Qu'Hoor.'

'Somer...is this true?' Her father looked so bewildered, and, yes, hurt, and Somer darted a bitter glance at Chase Lorimer. How dared he stand there so tall and confident, lying to her father? She wanted to deny what he had said. To throw his words back in his face, but her denial choked in her throat as she remembered his threats.

'Darling girl, why didn't you tell me you had fallen in love?' Sir Duncan chided gently. 'What an ogre you must think me to put my own comfort before your happiness. Of course you mustn't come with me.'

'I knew you'd understand, Sir Duncan.' Satisfaction gleamed in Chase's green eyes. 'And you mustn't blame Somer too much, for not telling you about us.' He reached out and grasped Somer's hand before she could evade him, carrying her fingers to his lips. 'Forgive me, darling,' he murmured huskily, 'I know what we agreed, but when it came to it, I just couldn't let you go. I fell in love with her five years ago in Jersey, but she ran away before I could tell her so,' Chase continued to her father, much as though Somer wasn't there, 'and then we bumped into one another several months ago.'

'And this time she didn't run,' Sir Duncan said, directing a brief smile at Somer.

'This time I didn't let her,' Chase corrected. 'Why don't you go and pour all three of us a drink, my darling, while I try to convince your father that I'm able to take proper care of you.'

'Chase, we're expecting people for dinner at any moment,' Somer began stiffly. Whatever she had expected when she had sent him her note it hadn't been this. No doubt this was his way of making it impossible for her to change her mind, she thought bitterly, and to judge from her father's reaction, although his announcement had stunned him, he was also quite pleased.

'Somer's godparents in actual fact,' Sir Duncan told Chase. 'You must join us, I'm sure they'll be as surprised by your announcement as I was. Somer, you should have told me,' he continued reproachfully. 'She always did have an over-active conscience,' he added to Chase. 'Why don't you come into my study, er…?'

'Chase, Chase Lorimer,' Chase supplied promptly.

'Of course,' Somer heard her father murmuring as he ushered his guest down the passage which led to his own private sanctum. 'Television West you're with, aren't you? You've done very well there by all accounts, turned it round in six months.'

Chase turned to follow her father, and Somer hissed bitterly at him, 'I suppose you think you're very clever, turning up here like this.'

'Just making sure that…' He bent his head swiftly, taking her half-parted lips in a hard kiss, releasing her almost as quickly.

Her breath exploded in her lungs, her eyes spitting fire

at him until she realised her father was watching them in amusement.

'Sorry about that,' Chase apologised without a trace of real regret, 'but it has been a very long time...'

'Almost twenty-four hours,' Somer agreed with mock sweetness.

'One thousand, four hundred and forty minutes,' Chase agreed with a theatrical sigh. 'I know, I've counted every one of them.'

CHAPTER FIVE

'AND now, I think the time has come for me to make a rather special announcement.'

In her chair opposite Chase and next to her father, Somer's fingers toyed nervously with the stem of her fluted champagne glass, knowing what was coming. She had already seen the covert looks Peter and Moira had been exchanging ever since they had arrived, and had no difficulty in tracing them to Chase's unexpected presence.

'SO, WHEN ARE YOU going to be married?' Somer was sitting next to Moira in the drawing-room trying to answer the older woman's excited questions with as much composure as she could muster.

'Oh I...'

'Just as soon as it can be arranged. I'm not giving her any opportunity to change her mind.'

Somer jumped nervously, spilling some of her coffee. She hadn't heard Chase approach and cursed him mentally just as she had been doing all evening.

'Well, you certainly kept him a secret,' Moira commented when Chase moved away to talk to Somer's father. 'I had no idea there was anyone serious.'

'I...that is we haven't known one another very long,' Somer mumbled awkwardly. She had never been a good liar and she bitterly resented the insidious position she now found herself in. She was uncomfortably aware of the puzzled and slightly hurt glances her father gave her from time to time, no doubt wondering why she had not confided in him. Why on earth had Chase come here tonight? She would have preferred to tell her father in her own way.

'I don't think one needs a long time when it's love,' Moira surprised her by saying. 'I knew the moment I met Peter. I think your new fiancé is rather impatient to have you to himself,' she added with a mischievous smile, 'so I'll go and join your father and Peter.'

As she left Chase took her place. The settee was only a small one and Somer found herself shrinking back automatically as she felt the warmth of his body brush against hers.

'We're supposed to be in love—remember?' Chase murmured the words softly against her ear.

'Why did you come here tonight?' Somer demanded. 'I wanted to tell my father myself.'

'Did you?'

The mocking disbelief in his eyes enraged her. 'Yes, I did,' she said grittily, 'but now that you are here, I want one thing to be clearly understood right from the start.'

'Yes?'

'I want your confirmation that our marriage will be strictly in name only.'

There was a curiously intense silence during which Somer could not summon the courage to look at him, and then to her chagrin he laughed. 'Oh I'm sure I can manage to restrain myself on that score, but...'

'Yes?' Somer demanded sharply.

'What I ask myself, my sweet,' Chase drawled lazily, 'is can you?'

Her eyes mirrored her shocked fury, but the biting pressure of his fingers closed around hers warned against voicing it. Peter and Moira were preparing to leave and Somer walked with her father to the door to see them off. 'I'm so thrilled for you,' Moira whispered as she kissed Somer's cheek. 'He's just the sort of man you need, Somer. Now don't forget to let me know the date of the wedding.'

Chase was still in the drawing-room, but as her father closed the front door, she hesitated, conscious of the need to say something to him, and yet still too angry with Chase to trust herself not to betray the truth to her father, albeit accidentally, once they started to talk.

'Moira's right,' he surprised her by saying, with a brief smile. 'He is right for you. You need a strong man, Somer. All the MacDonald women do.'

'Someone who'll beat me regularly once a day and twice on Sundays,' Somer said acidly.

To her relief her father chuckled, and then added more soberly, 'No, what you need is a man who is mentally strong because you have such strength yourself. If you picked a weak man sooner or later you'd start to despise him. You need a man you can respect, Somer. I think you've chosen well.'

A man she could respect! If only he knew. She wanted to laugh and cry at the same time.

'I like him,' Sir Duncan continued. 'Although I must say it's come as something of a shock. You should have told me.'

'I wasn't sure how serious Chase was.' The lie seemed to stick in her throat, but it was for her father's sake that she was doing this; that she was committing herself to this charade of a marriage, she reminded herself bitterly. If he started to suspect something now. 'And by the time I realised that he was...'

'Yes, I did rather get the impression he's rushing you off your feet a little. This marriage is what you want, isn't it?' He paused and looked thoughtfully at her. 'You are quite sure that he's the one?'

'Yes.' The lie whispered past her lips.

'Come on then, we'd better get back to the drawing-room before he thinks I'm coaxing you to change your mind. You mustn't worry about not coming to Qu'Hoor. The Government is providing me with a secretary-cum-aide, a young man who comes highly recommended.'

Chase was still sitting on the settee when they walked back into the drawing-room, and Somer had no option but to go and sit beside him while her father poured them all a final drink.

'To you both,' he toasted, raising his own glass. 'I hope you find as much happiness in your marriage as I did in mine.' He finished his drink, replacing his glass on a small table. 'And now I think I'll go up to bed.' His eyes twinkled. 'I'm sure you two have plenty to talk about.'

Chase stood up and the two men shook hands. Looking at him no one would guess the means he had used to force this engagement on her. He appeared the epitome of a man very much in love, right down to the way his eyes slid from her father's face to hers, Somer reflected sardonically. She would be wise to remember that her future husband was an accomplished actor.

'Would you like another drink before you leave?' Somer asked jerkily when the door had closed behind her father. All at once the atmosphere in the drawing-room was infused with a subtle tension. The tiny hairs on her arms prickled warningly, her throat was dry and tense.

'Always the gracious hostess,' Chase mocked, 'and no, I would not like another drink. I only stayed because your father expected it. No doubt right now he thinks the pair of us are in each other's arms taking full advantage of our privacy, although you hardly put on a convincing show of a woman deeply in love this evening.'

'Perhaps because I'm not as accomplished at deception as you obviously are,' Somer responded tautly, standing up and moving away from him to stand and face the window looking out on to the dark garden.

The warm breath stirring the hair at the back of her neck alerted her to his presence, her whole body going tight with apprehension. She hadn't heard him approach and wished he would go away.

'Then you'll just have to learn, won't you,' he mocked softly.

'Not if you're the one doing the teaching.'

'Oh.' His voice was silky smooth. 'I seem to remember there was a time when you were most anxious to take advantage of my...experience.'

Hot colour bloomed on Somer's pale skin. 'You enjoy reminding me about that, don't you?' she seethed furiously. 'You must love throwing it back in my face. It gives you almost as big a kick as rejecting me did in the first place.'

'If you say so.' He sounded bored, indifferent almost, and Somer whirled round to face him, checking when she saw how close this brought her to his body. There was only an inch or so between them, and she could feel the panicky sensation returning. Fear held her immobile, tremulous and breathing unevenly beneath his slow appraisal of her.

'Please leave,' she managed at last. 'I'm sure we've been down here long enough to convince my father that...'

'That I'm making love to you?' Chase taunted, his mouth twisting slightly. 'That isn't why I stayed.'

'Then...'

'I stayed to give you this.' He reached into his pocket

and produced a small leather box, flicking the lid open and removing the contents. Somer gasped when she caught the brilliant flash of sapphires and diamonds.

'Give me your hand.'

Her fingers curled away from him in mute protest. It suddenly seemed a sacrilege to let him put the ring on her finger; a betrayal of all that she had believed in and hoped for, but he was already grasping her fingers and uncurling them, sliding the silver and blue flashing band on to her finger, imprisoning her in the web of deceit he had spun round her.

'It fits.' She murmured the words more to herself than him, startled when he laughed, a warm pleasant sound.

'I told the jeweller you had long slender hands.' He was still holding one of those hands imprisoned within his and before Somer could stop him he raised it to his lips, lazily uncurling her tense fingers and dropping a light kiss in her palm. Dark lashes shadowed his eyes, an ache of pain rising up inside her as she dwelt on the mockery of his action. The dark lashes flicked up and he caught the look before she could hide it.

'What's the matter?'

'I hate what you're making me do. I hate you!'

'But once you wanted me to make love to you. You wanted me to take your virginity,' he reminded her softly. 'But it wasn't me you wanted, was it, Somer? It was just a man—any man.' He laughed in softly savage satisfaction as his words hit home. 'Ah yes, my dear, remember that when you feel like letting me know how much you despise me. Did the man who eventually took your virginity from you know that that was all he was; just a man?'

'Get out…get out…'

She couldn't remember the last time she had felt so bitterly angry. She could feel it boiling up inside her in a red-hot, blinding tide, so all encompassing that she didn't even realise Chase had gone until she heard the door close behind him. She glanced down at her hand, hating the precious stones glittering there. She was committed now, committed and trapped, and all because she had once, foolishly and naïvely, trusted him. Well, she had learned her lesson; she would never trust him or any other man again.

MUCH TO Somer's surprise and irritation Chase had opted for a church wedding, and although initially they had agreed on a very small number of guests, the list had grown and grown until it contained fifty-odd names. They were fortunate in that Sir Duncan's London home was large enough to hold all the guests for the reception. Outside caterers had been engaged, and Somer had found herself drawn unwillingly into discussions concerning what flowers to decorate the house and church with; what menu should be chosen, and a hundred and one other small details. At least they helped to keep her occupied, she thought tiredly, one half of her mind listening to what Moira was saying, the other running round in terrified circles, unable to believe that this time tomorrow she would be Chase Lorimer's wife. Her dress hung in her room carefully protected by a dust-sheet. The hairdresser was calling in the morning. The cake had arrived and Mrs McLeod was busily engaged in checking china and glass. Her father had thrown himself into the venture with considerable enthusiasm, insisting that he wanted her to have the sort of wedding she would always remember—how could he know that it was something she would only want to forget—and two MacDonald cousins had been press-ganged into acting as her bridesmaids. The whole thing was a ridiculous farce and try as she could she couldn't accept that she was one of its central figures. It seemed as though she were engaged on making all these arrangements for some-one else; that another girl was going to wear that white dress hanging in her room; and that that other girl would be the one walking down the aisle to meet Chase Lorimer.

THE MORNING of the wedding dawned fine and clear. So-mer seemed to move through the day like someone in a dream. By eleven o'clock she was longing for just five minutes to herself, to such an extent that she felt that she wanted to scream. She seemed to be surrounded by people fussing over her, the effort of maintaining her role as the happy, excited bride so much of a strain she had had to force back the desire to scream, 'I don't love him, I hate him and I don't want to marry him.'

Mrs McLeod and Moira helped her into her dress, a misty froth of white chiffon. She drove with her father to the church without seeing a single thing outside the car windows. Her fingers were as cold as ice, but the rest of her body seemed to be burning, consumed by fierce heat that made her dizzy and unable to concentrate. Everything seemed to be happening to her at a distance, as though she were enclosed in a protective bubble which no one but she could see. The interior of the church was cool after the heat outside. The walk down the aisle seemed to last for-ever, but at last it was over, and the vicar was sonorously intoning the words of the marriage service. Somer made her responses in a voice devoid of emotion, blank with despair and disbelief that this could actually be happening.

Chase took her hand to slide his ring on to her finger. His flesh felt warm and firm in stark contrast to the icy shivers of her own. At last it was over and they were back outside. Cameras flashed, the bright light bursting through her bubble and leaving her feeling intensely raw and vul-

erable. Where before everything had slid distantly by her,
ow she was acutely aware of her surroundings; of the
ood humour of the guests, so much at odds with her own
eelings; and most of all of Chase, tall and distinguished
t her side, smiling as he responded to people's good-
atured teasing. A tall dark woman who looked oddly fa-
niliar detached herself from a family group and came forward.

'My sister Helena,' Chase introduced blandly.

'I suppose the reason we never got to meet her before
oday was that you didn't want to put her off,' Helena
oked, smiling down at Somer. She was tall with Chase's
eatures cast in much softer mould, but her eyes were blue
nstead of green. Even so, Somer felt herself withdrawing
lightly from her, frightened of what she might read in her
eyes. 'Has he told you yet?' she asked with a smile.

'Told me?' Involuntarily Somer's eyes widened, her
ace turning queryingly up to Chase's.

Helena grinned gleefully. 'Have a look over there,' she
nvited Somer, waving her hand in the direction of the
group she had just left.

Weakly Somer did so, she saw a pleasant-looking
sandy-haired man in his late thirties and...her eyes widened fractionally as she saw two sets of identical faces, all
of them bearing a strong resemblance to Chase and Helena,
although one pair had sandy hair and the other brown.

'It runs in the family,' Helena told her succinctly. 'Our
parents were warned and stopped at one pair of twins. John
and I thought we could beat the odds, and ended up with
two; Chase always used to say he wanted to go for the
treble.'

'You two are twins?'

Helena looked at her brother in grinning appreciation.
'Ah...ha, so you didn't tell her. Didn't want to give her

the opportunity to back out, I suppose. There've bee
twins in our family for the last five generations,' she tol
Somer with a grin, adding with relish, 'and so far no one'
escaped. I wonder what you're going to get—mixed dou
bles or a matching pair?'

'Hasn't it occurred to you that your surmises are a trifl
indelicate, seeing we're only just married?' Chase re
marked. His arm was resting against the back of Somer'
waist, his fingers curling round her hip, and Somer trie
to move away, overpowered by the sheer masculinity o
him. Every time she tried to draw a breath she seemed t
breathe in the male scent of him, her senses acutely height
ened and aware of him in a way which was extremel
disturbing.

'Indelicate?' Helena laughed. 'When did that ever worr
you? And when are you coming down to see us? The kid
have missed you.'

'When we come back from our honeymoon.'

'So when do you plan to move into Barnwell?'

'Just as soon as we're ready.'

'Has he taken you to see it yet?' she asked Somer. 'Un
cle Charles became something of a recluse as he got older
I used to go over and see him, but he didn't like visitors
The house is basically solid enough but the furnishings…
She pulled a wry face. 'Still, Chase is well off enough fo
you to put it all right. Do you work at all?'

'I write computer programmes,' Somer told her, 'but it'
very spasmodic and of course I can work from home.' She
felt rather than saw Chase frowning, and Helena who had
seen it too laughed.

'What's the matter, big brother?' she mocked. 'Don'
you like the thought of an independent wife? He's the mos
terrible chauvinist,' she told Somer with relish. 'You
wouldn't believe how bossy he was as a kid and all be-

cause he was ten minutes older than me. Don't let him push you around. Like all men he enjoys the thought of having his wife all helpless and dependent on him.'

'John, will you please take her away,' he implored his brother-in-law mock defeatedly. Up until then Somer hadn't felt the slightest twinge of curiosity about Chase's background. It came as a shock to discover that he had this other side to him; that he was so plainly idolised by Helena's two sets of twins, the four boys deluging him with questions until their parents shooed them away.

'And I did so want at least one daughter,' Helena mourned, watching them disappear in the direction of the buffet table, 'but John says his nerves won't stand another try. Still,' she brightened up perceptibly, 'if I had a niece or two…'

'Take her away, John,' Chase drawled, adding to Somer for the benefit of his family, 'you have the most illuminating expression, darling. I could almost see you blenching at the thought of a couple of Amazons like my boisterous sister…'

'Children…children…' John's mild voice teased them. He and Chase moved slightly away to talk about a business deal John was setting up, leaving the two women alone. 'Seriously, I'm very fond of my brother,' Helena said bluntly.

'I expect you were very surprised when you heard about us getting married.'

'Not once I'd seen you,' was Helena's cryptic response. 'I recognised you from your photograph,' she added. 'Chase had a bad bout of tropical fever when he came back from Jersey—it's a recurring thing he gets when he overworks. He was staying with us at the time, and I unpacked his case for him. The photographs were in it. I guessed then how he felt about you, although we never talked about it—twins don't need to.'

Helena thought that Chase loved her! Somer opened her mouth to tell her exactly why she was marrying her beloved brother, and how he had compelled her to do so, and closed it again, impelled by some emotion she scarcely understood not to destroy Helena's illusions.

Ten minutes later when Chase was back at her side, she bitterly regretted her magnanimity.

'I hope you've told her how lovely she looks, Chase,' Helena commented, before going to rejoin her husband. 'I know people always say the bride looks beautiful, but this one really does. That dress is a dream,' she added to Somer before moving away.

At last the speeches and cake-cutting were over, and it was time for them to slip away.

'Where are we going?' Somer asked Chase curtly before she went upstairs to change.

'It's a surprise, but I've taken Mrs McLeod into my confidence and I understand she's packed a case for you.'

When she went up to her room Somer discovered this to be true. Moira was waiting for her, and had a pretty linen suit laid out on her bed. It was one Somer hadn't worn before, its pale lemon colour bringing out the blue-black lights in her hair and emphasising the delicacy of her skin. She was ready with five minutes to spare, which was more to Moira's credit than to her own. Chase knocked on her door and then walked into her room just as she was putting the finishing touches to her make-up. Their eyes met in the mirror and Somer felt herself colour up as her hand trembled betrayingly.

'I'll take your case down,' Chase murmured easily. 'You've got five minutes.'

'Or you'll do what? Leave without me?'

Moira laughed, not noticing the murderously cold glance the newly married pair exchanged.

Downstairs they had to run the gauntlet of well-wishers. Somer kissed and hugged her father. He was leaving for Qu'Hoor at the end of the month. For the first time it hit her that she was leaving her home for good; that she would be sharing the home of a man who was virtually a stranger to her; a man she loathed and despised, and who had tricked her into this travesty of a marriage for his own purposes.

Chase helped her into his car, a silver-grey Mercedes, and then slid into the driver's seat. The traffic blurred round them as Somer tried to concentrate on calming her overwrought nerves. They had gone several miles before she recognised the route. They were going to Heathrow.

Chase parked the car and helped her out of it. 'I've arranged for someone to pick it up later. This way.'

The departure lounge was thronged with people as might be expected during the peak holiday season. Somer felt tired and drained, barely glancing round her as she followed Chase. Like a dog with a new master, she thought bitterly, watching the way in which the crowds seemed to part automatically to let him through, while she was swallowed up in his wake. The girl handling passenger arrivals gave him a dazzling smile and Somer felt a painful twinge seize her middle. Indigestion, she told herself solidly, looking away.

'Your flight will be boarding shortly, sir,' the girl told Chase with another admiring smile. 'If you'll just weigh in your luggage.' Somer glanced indifferently at the departures board. It mattered little to her where they went, and then she felt as though her stomach were plunging crazily downwards, like a lift suddenly out of control.

'Jersey,' she accused Chase huskily, 'we're going to Jersey?'

'Why not? I thought it the romantically appropriate choice.'

Somer's fingers dug into her palms. It was the only way she could stop herself from screaming at him. Oh, he had chosen Jersey deliberately all right, but not for any romantic reasons. No, he wanted to underline the hold he had over her; he wanted to torment her with the past, with her folly in believing that… That what? That she was desirable enough for a man to want to make love to her? The very way in which he agreed that their marriage should be in name only had proved how undesirable he found her, and yet he obviously believed that she had had lovers. And she would make sure that he continued to think so. How he would mock her if he knew the truth; if he knew that after his rejection she hadn't allowed any man close enough to her for it to happen again.

'Would you like a cup of coffee or something before we board?' Somer nodded briefly, anything to get rid of him, to be alone for a few precious minutes.

'No running out on me, Somer,' he warned tautly. 'Because if you do I'll only come after you.'

Where could she run to? Back to her father who believed that she and Chase were deeply in love? Somer sat down and leaned back in her seat closing her eyes, unaware of how pale and fragile she looked beneath the artificial lighting. Mauve shadows lay under her eyes, her skin pulled tightly over the high cheekbones.

They boarded in mutual silence, Somer taking the window seat Chase proffered even though she didn't want it. She closed her eyes automatically as they took off, her fingers instinctively groping for and finding Chase's. When they were safely airborne and her panic was over she tugged her hand away tensely. 'Well, well, you do have some human tendencies after all. I was beginning to think I'd married a robot.'

'You married someone you could get rid of in twelve months so that you could claim your inheritance,' Somer reminded him, 'and you blackmailed me into marrying you.'

'So I did, and perhaps if you're very good I'll reward you with a nice cheque the day our divorce becomes final.'

'The only reward I want is the return of those negatives...'

'Ah yes, those.' He smiled mockingly at her. 'How you've changed. You've become so cold and hard I barely recognise you. What happened?'

How dared he ask her that after the way he'd rejected her? 'You should know,' she spat out angrily without thinking.

'Should I?' The green eyes narrowed and studied her closely. 'Oh, you mean you could hardly be expected to retain the air of innocence I remembered when you've slipped in and out of as many beds as you must have, although curiously you've managed to convince the gossip columnists that you're whiter than white. Very clever of you. How do you do it?'

To Somer's relief the stewardess came round asking if they would like a drink before Chase could goad her any more and shortly after that came the announcement they would soon be landing.

Chase had arranged a hire car which was waiting for them at the airport. Somer felt the same indefinable tension which had gripped her at the reception, coiling through her as they set out for the hotel.

'Where are we staying?' she asked casually, dreading

hearing the answer. 'Where do you think?' Chase shot her a mocking look. 'Only this time we'll be sharing.'

'The Hermitage?' Her voice was dry and husky.

'Where else? Romantic of me, wasn't it? Perhaps we'll even return to that beach and...'

'Stop it!' Somer gripped the sides of her seat, her face white with anguish.

'What's the matter?' Chase drawled. 'Don't you like being reminded of how we first met? Or is it something else you'd rather not remember, Somer? How many men did you have to beg to make love to you until you found one that was willing?'

He might just as well have struck her physically, the effect was much the same. She winced away from him, her eyes almost black with shock and pain.

'You bastard,' she said hoarsely, reaching blindly for the door handle, not thinking beyond her overpowering need to escape not only from Chase but from her own thoughts as well.

The car screeched to a halt as Chase braked and pulled off the road, his face white with temper as he reached across her gripping her shoulders. 'You crazy little fool,' he grated, shaking her. 'What the hell were you trying to do? Kill yourself?'

'Why should that bother you? I should think it would be the perfect solution to all your problems, you wouldn't even need to wait twelve months to get rid of me that way,' Somer retaliated wildly.

Suddenly the pressure of Chase's grip slackened a little, his mouth a grim line as he studied her flushed face and too-bright eyes. 'This is crazy,' he muttered, withdrawing one hand to push it irately through his hair. 'We can't go on baiting one another like this.'

'We?' Somer allowed her eyebrows to lift in chilling disdain.

'You don't exactly turn the other cheek,' Chase reminded her silkily, 'but I suggest we try to call a truce—at least for the time being. We're supposed to be on our honeymoon—remember?'

'Only when I have to,' Somer retorted without thinking, watching the anger darken and narrow his eyes. 'All right,' she agreed weakly. 'I agree—let's have a truce by all means. Does the hotel know...I mean...?'

'Do they know we're a honeymoon couple?' Chase finished sardonically for her. 'No. And I've booked us a suite,' he added, comprehensively, 'with two bedrooms, so you'll be quite safe.'

'I never doubted that for a moment,' Somer responded tartly, not liking the amusement in his eyes. The Hermitage. Did Andrew still work there?

How strange it was that while her thoughts had returned to Chase many many times during the intervening years, she had rarely thought about Andrew, and yet he had been the one she had been engaged to; the one whose defection and rejection she ought to have felt the most. Instead it had been Chase she had dreamed of during those awful nightmares when she cried and clung to him, begging him to make love to her and he pushed her away, turning his back on her, walking away from her...

'What's the matter now?'

'Nothing.' Her response was clipped and short. She glanced up just in time to see Chase bending towards her, and read the purpose in his eyes panicking and trying to turn away, but it was too late. Lean fingers cupped her jaw, curving along the bone and holding her prisoner, his breath warm against her skin. It was impossible to tear her glance from his, and the pulse in her throat jerked spasmodically as she tried to control her breathing.

His mouth brushed hers, cool and firm, registering the betraying quiver of her lips. She tensed and drew back from him. 'Why did you do that?' she began huskily. 'We agreed…'

'Why?' His softly amused voice cut across her protest, his thumb probing the vulnerable curve of her lips. 'Perhaps it was because you looked so…hungry.'

He couldn't have said anything more calculated to bring her back to earth. Her body tensed back against her seat, her eyes flashing bitter fire.

'If I am it isn't a hunger that you could satisfy,' she threw at him ignoring the danger signals leaping to life in his eyes. 'I don't want you touching me, Chase Lorimer, I don't want you kissing me, and I…'

His mouth closed on hers with devastating intensity, forcing her into silence beneath its crushing pressure.

When Somer eventually managed to wrench her head away her senses were swimming. Darkly purple eyes glared with impotent fury into taunting green.

'I just thought we'd better seal our pact before hostilities broke out again,' Chase murmured smoothly, adding with silky determination, 'and if you give in to that fierce MacDonald temper your father assures me you have and try to hit me, I promise you you'll regret it.'

'No real man ever hits a woman,' Somer retaliated scornfully, dredging up something she had once heard said.

'Who said anything about hitting,' Chase drawled softly, 'and be very careful about questioning my manhood, Somer. I might take it as a challenge that overrides any agreement about the consummation of our marriage.'

The thought of his possession of her fuelled by the cold pride she could see glittering in his eyes brought a weak shudder to her body. She turned away, almost sagging with relief when she heard him re-start the car.

'Sensible of you, if somewhat unexpected,' Chase taunted as he drove on, and somewhere deep down in her subconscious Somer felt the suspicion stir that he might have deliberately provoked her angry response to him so that it would give him an excuse to…to make love to her? Hardly that. To afford him another opportunity to humiliate her? She shook her head, muzzily disturbed by thoughts too complicated for her to unravel in her present exhausted state. All she wanted to do right now was take a shower and then fall into bed. How nice it would be when she woke up if she were to discover that Chase Lorimer and her marriage to him were both merely bad dreams.

CHAPTER SIX

THE foyer had been decorated since Somer last visited the hotel and was now coolly attractive in crisp green and white with white cane furniture and banked displays of plants. She didn't recognise either of the girls behind the reception desk, and mocked herself for her tiny sigh of relief. Andrew and Judith must surely have been transferred to another hotel years ago if indeed they were still working for the same chain. Once it had been her ambition for Andrew to see her with Chase; to realise that even if he did not want her, other men did, but now...

'Somer?'

She hadn't realised he was watching her, the dark brows drawn together in query as he searched her face.

'Re-living old memories?' he asked her as he guided her towards the lift. His question caught her by surprise, her eyes widening. 'Perhaps he was the one you lost your virginity to?'

'I don't want to talk about it.' She wasn't going to tell Chase that after that afternoon with him she had left the hotel without seeing Andrew again.

'Why? Not still nursing an adolescent crush on him, are you?'

'And if I am? Don't they say that a woman always re-members her first lover? That he always holds a very special place in her heart.'

As she said the words it struck Somer with a sickeningly

illuminating blow that Chase was the closest thing she had ever had to a lover, and that he was the one she remembered—not Andrew. Chase was the one who haunted those feverishly unhappy dreams that still tormented her.

'Stop thinking about him.' The harsh command splintered her thoughts, her face turning automatically in obedience to it. The lift stopped, the doors opened, depositing them on a floor of the hotel she hadn't visited before. Thick, expensive carpet muffled the sound of their footsteps. Three doors opened off the square foyer, each one bearing a discreet plaque. 'Versailles Suite' Somer read on the door Chase was opening. Thank God he hadn't booked a bridal suite, was the hysterical thought as she preceded him through the open door.

She was in an elegant sitting-room, with huge patio windows and a view over the sea that made her gasp her pleasure out loud. Outside the windows was a small terrace equipped with a wrought-iron table and four chairs. Two other doors led off the sitting-room, and Chase gestured towards them.

'I believe both bedrooms are the same, take whichever one you want. Would you like a drink?' He walked over to the small bar and removed two glasses while Somer hesitated, glancing towards the bedroom doors and then back at the tall dark man who was now her husband. The word was like a cold shock of water icing down her spine.

'No thanks,' she responded coolly, opening the nearer of the doors. 'I'm rather tired. It's been a long day. I'd like to shower and then rest.'

A mocking smile twisted Chase's lips. 'Of course,' he agreed suavely, 'I understand completely.'

He picked up his glass and headed for the patio doors, unfastening the catch and sliding them open. The dying sun caught his strong profile, his dark hair ruffled by the light breeze, thick strands curling over the collar of his shirt. Just for a moment Somer remembered what it felt like to touch, crisp and yet soft; she could almost smell the clean scent of him; feel his body heat, and she shuddered, trying to dispel the sensation of bleak emptiness possessing her. Why did she stand by her bedroom door, her body trembling with the onset of a strange weakness, wishing that somehow things might have been different, that…

No! The denial exploded silently inside her giving her the motivation to walk into her room. It was as attractively furnished as the sitting-room, in shades of peach and rust. The double bed seemed to taunt her and she averted her eyes from it as she explored her surroundings. Her window overlooked the sea too and shared the sitting-room's patio. Another door opened into a private bathroom decorated to match her bedroom. The round sunken bath made her eyes widen. It was easily large enough for two people and the startlingly erotic images that suddenly came to mind brought hot colour to her face.

It took a considerable effort of willpower to bathe in the sunken bath and at the same time keep at bay those taunting mental images of Chase's body, brown and sleekly muscled, his hands touching her skin… Somer became aware of an ache in the pit of her stomach, a restless urgency that needed no definition. She left her bath hurriedly, wrapping herself in one of the large soft towels and walking back into her bedroom. Someone had brought up her luggage. Her case was on a chair. Apart from her own movements the suite was completely silent. Chase must have gone out. The knowledge should have pleased her, but in reality what she felt was a searing sense of desertion. What was the matter with her, she wondered in self-disgust. She was behaving like…like a frustrated spinster out of a dubious novel. Why of all people did Chase Lorimer have to come back into her life again? Why couldn't he have left her alone? She knew the answer to that question, she reminded herself as she unpacked her case—all too well.

Half an hour later Chase had still not returned, and despite her tiredness Somer knew she would not sleep. Quickly pulling on a pair of jeans and a tee-shirt she left the suite without bothering to glance in her mirror, her hair a dark, unconfined cloud on her shoulders, her eyes dark and stormy with emotion.

This time there were more people in the foyer—it was late afternoon and people were returning from the beach to prepare for dinner. Somer glanced in the bar, but there was no sign of Chase. What was she doing looking for him anyway, she had no desire for his company.

Angry with herself for the emotions which threatened to get out of control, she headed for the main door, half colliding with someone as she did so. Masculine hands gripped her shoulders, a stunned, 'Somer' exhaled by her ear. She looked up, recognition replacing her frown.

'Andrew! Good heavens, I didn't think you'd still be here.'

'No?' An amused smile curved the lips she had once fantasised about so hectically. The years had not been as kind to Andrew as they had to Chase, Somer noticed with a remarkable degree of satisfaction. Andrew's fair hair had thinned noticeably, and although his skin was healthily tanned the body she remembered as lean and fit had thickened and become almost paunchy. 'Then what *are* you doing here?'

It took several seconds for it to sink into her consciousness that Andrew thought she was at the hotel because of him. Once the knowledge would have made her tongue-tied with embarrassment, now she was merely amazed at his self-conceit.

'I'm on holiday,' she told him with a cool smile. Was this really the man she had wanted to commit her life to? She glanced up into the rather too well assured face and sent up a mental prayer of fervent gratitude to Judith Barnes. But for her she might have ended up married to Andrew.

'Alone?'

'Oh no…not alone,' she told him with a smile. 'Actually I'm here with my husband.' She was enjoying this, she realised dizzily, enjoying watching the betraying expressions following one another across Andrew's too easily read face.

'So you're married.' He reached for her hand, examining her rings and sighing faintly. 'If I hadn't been such a fool you would have been married to me.'

'Perhaps.' Her smile was deliberately non-committal, 'Although I doubt whether many girls marry the first man they fall in love with.'

'I've never forgiven myself for hurting you the way I did.'

'You would have hurt me far more if I'd found out about Judith after we were married. What happened to her, by the way? Did the pair of you ever make it to the Caribbean, or couldn't you find someone else as gullible as I was?'

'It was all a mistake,' he muttered thickly. 'I just *told* Judith that I didn't want you.'

'You mean you lied to both of us?' She gave him a sweetly mocking smile. 'I'm not eighteen any more, Andrew, and I'm afraid that line just won't work.' She glanced up as someone else walked into the foyer, her heart thumping as she saw Chase strolling towards them. For some reason she felt an urgent desire to tug her hand away from Andrew's, rather like a guilty child, which was surely foolish as it couldn't matter in the slightest to Chase what she did.

'So there you are, darling.' He came straight towards them, the pressure of his hand on her waist, tugging her away from Andrew who was forced to release her. 'Aren't you going to introduce us?'

She did so, watching the way they studied one another, like two wary animals.

'So this is your husband,' Andrew said at length. 'I'm glad you found someone. I've always hated myself for hurting you the way I did. Somer and I were once engaged,' he added in brief explanation to Chase while Somer held her breath. Andrew was deliberately trying to cause trouble. For all he knew she might never have mentioned him to Chase. She glanced into the dark, shuttered face of her husband. There was nothing to betray any reaction, but Chase obviously knew what was going on.

'Yes, I believe she mentioned it to me,' he agreed smoothly. 'She found you in bed with someone else, didn't she?'

Andrew went bright red. The look he gave Chase was bitterly angry, and Somer found herself moving automatically between them, her fingers curling round Chase's muscular forearm. Green eyes searched her pale face.

'I thought you were going to rest.' He said it abruptly, leaving her feeling like a chastised child.

'I couldn't sleep. I didn't know where you'd gone.'

'And so you came looking for me?' He smiled suddenly, the smile transforming his features so much that she caught her breath in involuntary reaction. 'If I'd known you were going to miss me I'd never have gone.' The look in his eyes was almost a physical caress, and Somer knew she wasn't alone in recognising it as such. Andrew looked at her bleakly, and excused himself. Chase waited until he was out of earshot and then said softly, 'So that's him. No wonder you were so shocked when I told you we were staying here. Did you know he was still here?'

How could she tell him that she'd barely given Andrew a thought, and that the reason for her shock had been her memories of him? Pride wouldn't let her.

'I didn't know.'

'But you hoped?' His fingers tightened painfully on her upper arm. 'Well let's get one thing understood. There'll be no taking up where the pair of you left off. No matter what your life style might have been before, while you're married to me there'll be no lovers.'

'Andrew and I were never lovers.'

'Not for want of encouragement on your part,' Chase reminded her cruelly. 'Oh, yes, I can remember everything you told me, Somer, but there'll be no consummation of your adolescent fantasies this time round either. If you want a lover that badly…'

'I don't,' Somer cut in bitterly, shaking her arm free of his grip and hurrying back to the lift. Chase was behind her, but there were other people in the lift and he could say nothing to her while they were present. If she wanted a lover that badly. His cold words rang tormentingly in her ears, her fists clenched in mute anger at her sides. What did it matter what he thought? Wasn't it better that he thought her promiscuous than run the risk of his discovering the truth? That since his rejection of her she hadn't been able to endure the trauma of the same thing happening again. That every time a date had so much as kissed her, she had remembered his kisses, his touch, and then his withdrawal leaving her aching and bereft.

They entered the suite in a heavy silence filled with unspoken tension. Somer pushed open the patio doors, moving restlessly on to the terrace, unwilling to face Chase, and yet too proud to run for the sanctuary of her own room.

'I meant what I said, Somer. Any attempt to rekindle that old affair and I'll…'

'You'll what?' She turned towards him, her eyes brilliant with pain and unshed tears. 'I'm tired of your threats, Chase. You're nothing but a bully…'

She pushed past him before he could speak, locking her bedroom door and then leaning against it, dismayed to discover that she was trembling. Why had she spoken to him like that? They had declared a truce and yet what she had just done had come very close to goading him into…into what? she asked herself. Making love to her? Hadn't she learned her lesson the first time? She didn't want him; she *couldn't* want a man who had rejected her as cruelly as he had, and yet deep down inside herself she knew she was lying. She did want him. It appalled and dismayed her, but the truth had to be faced. Sitting on her bed she forced herself to think back, to remember… Her fears that her inexperience and gaucheness would put men off had been those of any shy adolescent until she met Chase. If she hadn't met him; if he hadn't rejected her she would have overcome them in time, but his rejection had been like a red-hot knife placed across an open wound, sealing it up for ever.

IT WAS A lovely day, Somer admitted as she breakfasted on the private terrace, but no amount of blue skies and bright sunshine could make up for the lack of pleasant companionship. Chase had already left the suite when she woke up. She had ordered her breakfast and showered, not knowing how she was going to spend the day. Presumably

the hire car was still parked outside. She could always g
for a drive. Some honeymoon!

She was just brushing her hair when she heard the knoc
on the outer door. Thinking it was the maid she called ou
'Come in,' but it was Andrew who opened the door, smi
ing at her. 'I saw that your husband was down to play gol
this morning and so I thought I'd come up and see if yo
fancied going out for a drive. It's my day off,' he adde
by way of explanation.

Mindful of Chase's warning she was just about to re
fuse, when a sudden spark of defiance took fire. 'All righ
I will come with you. Just give me five minutes to get m
things.'

'Bring a swimsuit,' Andrew called after her, his eye ad
miring her slender figure when she emerged from her roor
dressed in a brief white top and figure-hugging jeans. Fiv
years ago he had thought her too thin, but that thinnes
had changed to elegant slenderness, the briefness of he
cotton top emphasising the soft thrust of her breasts
Aware of the way he was looking at her a trickle of warn
ing slid down her spine but Somer ignored it. She coul
handle Andrew—hadn't she handled dozens of men lik
him in the last five years?

'All set? My car's parked round the park in the staff ca
park. I'll meet you out front if that's okay with you?'

Who didn't he want to see them together, Somer won
dered cynically, agreeing to his suggestion with a brie
smile. She had learned a lot in five years, including th
ability to see beneath surface statements.

Andrew's car was a small scarlet two-seater. Some
climbed into the passenger seat and fastened her belt, tuck
ing her bag on the floor beside her. As she did so her han
caught the glove compartment and it flew open revealin
a make-up bag and headscarf. They could have belonge

to anyone, but Somer sensed they were indications of a long-standing relationship.

'They're Judith's,' Andrew told her tersely. 'We got married just after you left—the worst mistake I ever made, but she was pregnant and she claimed the child was mine.'

Andrew hadn't changed, Somer thought idly. He was still looking for someone else to blame for his own mistakes. She felt almost sorry for Judith, even remembering the other woman's aggressive unpleasantness towards herself. Looking back she could quite understand it. Judith had loved Andrew, and perhaps even then suspected she might be carrying his child. She had seen Somer as a threat to that relationship; even while her greed had condoned Andrew's actions. They deserved one another, she thought wryly, and wondered with cynicism how many guests Andrew had been unfaithful to her with in the intervening five years.

They drove to a small, quiet beach and while Andrew parked the car Somer made her way down on to the sand, spreading out her towel and pulling off her jeans. Underneath she was wearing the bottom half of her bikini and by the time Andrew joined her she was smoothing oil into her legs.

'I'd have done that for you if you'd waited,' he told her huskily, admiring the long, slender length of her. 'Why don't you take off your top? The beach is quite private and we've got it all to ourselves.'

Somer smiled. 'My skin's too pale to risk too much sun at once. Perhaps later when I've built up a little resistance.'

Did he really think she was still as naïve as she had been at eighteen? Then she would have needed no urging. Then she would have been thrilled and proud to believe that he wanted her physically, now all she could feel was a brief cynicism for his obviousness, a tiny inner voice reminding her that what Andrew was really interested in wasn't her, but her father's wealth. He had never really wanted her.

It was late afternoon when they returned. Andrew insisted on escorting Somer back to the suite, and she let him, still cynically amused by his attempts to ingratiate himself back into her good books.

As he opened the door for her the first thing she realised was that Chase was back; the second was that there was someone with him and she stiffened in immediate hostility recognising Judith.

She had put on weight in the intervening years, but she was still attractive. Cold blue eyes shot bitter sparks of fury at Somer and Andrew.

'Now do you believe me,' she hissed furiously to Chase as Andrew closed the door behind them. 'I told you what was going on... I knew exactly what would happen the moment I knew she was back. She wanted Andrew five years ago, and nothing's changed. She still wants him.'

'Judith, come on...' Andrew interrupted awkwardly, walking to his wife's side. 'Somer is an old friend...it's all perfectly innocent.

'If the pair of you want to argue, I suggest you do so in your own quarters,' Chase cut in coldly, walking across to the door and holding it open. Andrew glanced helplessly across to Somer, his expression both pleased and rueful. He was enjoying the scene, Somer recognised—and so possibly in her own way was Judith.

'I suppose you enjoyed that,' Chase murmured with dangerous softness when they were alone. 'Tit for tat, so to speak. You certainly didn't waste much time.'

'Chase, please, you've got it all wrong...I had no idea that Andrew and Judith were married until this morning.'

'But knowing didn't stop you from going out with him?'

'Why should it?' Anger suddenly filled her. 'You don't own me, Chase. I didn't ask to marry you. You blackmailed me into it, and if I want to go out with Andrew…'

'Go to bed with him, don't you mean?' Chase snarled, his face so bitterly furious that she stepped back from him automatically. 'I warned you about that, Somer. But if you're so desperate for a man that you can't even go a few days without one, perhaps I ought to oblige you myself. That way at least I'll stop you breaking up someone else's marriage.'

'Chase, no.' Alarm sprang to life in her eyes, and she backed away hastily. 'Chase, you said this would be a marriage in name only. You can't…' She stifled a small cry as his fingers bit into her arms and he swung her off her feet, shouldering open his bedroom door. His room was a twin of her own but without the sea views. A double bed much like her own gave beneath their combined weight, Somer holding her arms rigid to fend Chase off, her body tensed for escape.

'This has nothing to do with our marriage, Somer,' Chase ground out as he reached for the hem of her tee-shirt. 'It's something I ought to have done five years ago.'

'Five years ago I came to you because…'

'Because you wanted someone to take the place of your fiancé.' The gritted comment seared her tender skin as Chase jerked her top upwards, stilling her thrashing body effortlessly as he pulled it over her head, leaving her feeling more exposed than she had ever felt in her life as his gaze scorched her pale skin. Her convulsive attempt to sit up and cross her arms over her breasts in their brief covering of white lace was punished by his fingers manacling her wrists together behind her. 'How many men have you used trying to forget him since?' He laughed harshly deep in his throat. 'You should be grateful to me, Somer—I'm going to make sure you forget him. This time my name will be the one you cry out at the summit of your pleasure,' he told her thickly. 'Mine.' His mouth closed hotly over hers, giving her no opportunity to respond, smothering her resistance with the thick blanket of power she could sense surging through him.

Confusing emotions exploded inside her. She wanted to fight against him, to freeze him off with the same cold lack of response she had shown to other men but her body was overruling her will, recognising and even welcoming his touch. Her breasts swelled, her nipples springing to urgent life inside their lacy prison, a hungry sound of need torn from her throat as Chase released her mouth, his thumb probing its swollen outlines, his fingers finding the catch that released her bra.

Somer struggled feebly to escape from the crushing grip of his fingers on her wrists, only realising how provocative her movements were when Chase muttered a harsh exclamation, his eyes almost black above cheekbones that burned with darkly aroused colour.

'You do things to me I thought I was far too experienced to feel,' he muttered against her jaw. His tongue burned a tantalising line down her throat, his free hand cupping one breast. Her nipples, tautly aroused and deeply pink against her white skin, thrust eagerly upwards, her tormented moan as Chase's thumb rubbed provocatively against one echoed by the fierce sound he made deep in his throat.

'Beautiful.' He muttered the word almost reverently bending his head until it was pressed against her. Her pinioned wrists were released, but Somer was beyond caring. The sight of his dark head against her breasts brought a deep shudder from her body, her fingers curling into his shoulders in mute need when his tongue traced a delicately spiralling pattern round one erect nipple.

A deep coiling sensation erupted in the pit of her stomach. Feverishly Somer tugged at his shirt buttons, sliding her hands over his warm moist flesh, shivering tensely when Chase muttered, 'Take it off, I want to feel you against me.'

Her fingers moved clumsily over the remaining buttons, her eyes unwittingly betraying her arousal as he thrust the shirt off. His skin was as tanned as she remembered, her own erotically pale in comparison. When his arms slid round her rib cage, pulling her tightly against him until his mouth rested against the curve of one breast her heart started to pound unsteadily. His hand stroked down over the curve of her waist and rested on her hip, his touch burning into her through the fabric of her jeans. As though unable to resist the temptation any longer her finger crept into the thick hair at the back of his neck, eliciting a growl of protest.

'Somer.' He groaned her name, roughly caressing her other breast, watching the quivers of pleasure run through her slender body with hungry appreciation. 'If you react like this with every man who touches you, you must drive them all mad. No wonder he wants you back.'

The words struck her like painful blows, reality intruding into the dream world of desire she had lost herself in.

'Chase, please, we mustn't do this...'

He laughed harshly, reaching for the zip of her jeans, and pulling it down. 'Very proper,' he mocked, 'but you want this as much as I do. Your body's aching to be made love to.' His hand rested intimately against her brief silk panties. Somer could feel the heat flooding through her and knew shamingly that what he said was true. An unfamiliar sensation spread through her, intensifying the coiling ache she had experienced earlier. She moved uneasily,

trying to edge away, but Chase's hand still rested possessively against the intimate core of her body.

'You want me to do this...' His green eyes seemed to
burn into her as he bent his head and found her breast
again, stroking her nipple with his tongue, 'and this.' His
hand moved and she gasped, struggling away from him in
shocked rejection, but knowing that he was right, and also
knowing how much more she wanted than merely his
touch.

'Come on, Somer, don't play games.' His voice was
rough with warning and something else she couldn't recognise. 'You aren't eighteen any longer, and if it's any
consolation to you, I want you just as much as you want
me, feel.' He reached for her hand and drew it against his
body, emitting a soft groan of pleasure as her fingers
brushed his tautly muscled thigh. She couldn't do this,
Somer's mind screamed in shocked protest, she did not
have the experience to cope with Chase's demands, but
once again her body overruled her mind, her pulse rate
climbing alarmingly as her body registered its own response to Chase's arousal.

'Somer, touch me...make love to me.' His lips burned
a fiery trail across her skin, burning the vulnerable skin of
her shoulder and throat, her body quiveringly responsive
to each kiss. 'Let me take these off.'

Chase stood up and removed his jeans. Somer felt her
throat go dry as she tried to drag her gaze away. She had
seen him like this before—well, almost, his underwear was
somewhat briefer and more revealing than his swimming
shorts had been and then five years ago he hadn't been so
obviously aroused. Unable to stop herself she reached out
tentatively, touching her fingertips to the hair-coarsened
flesh of his thigh. Lean fingers trapped the soft fluttering
of hers against his body.

'Somer.' He muttered her name as though he was fighting to breathe, and Somer quivered in instantaneous response. He really wanted her; he desired *her*. No one else. *Her*. An indescribable flood of sensation flooded through her, a heady, delirious delight that found expression in the tentative caress of her fingers within the imprisonment of his.

'Somer.' This time he wrenched them away from his body and carried them to his lips, kissing them lightly until his eyes suddenly darkened and he sucked their soft pink tips compulsively, pulling her back on to the bed with him. When he released her she was still shivering with a mingling of pleasure and almost unbearable tension.

'Take off your jeans.' She had barely registered the softly spoken command when Chase muttered, 'No…let me do it for you.' Her fingers clenched into her palms when she felt the warm brush of his mouth against her thigh as Chase removed her jeans, his fingers stroking seductively against her skin. 'You're so beautifully responsive,' he muttered thickly, coming to lie beside her, one hand resting possessively on her hip, his fingers fanning out against her skin. 'Normally with a woman of your experience one finds that her responses have been blunted…but with you…it's as though no man's ever touched you before.'

Warning bells rang in Somer's brain. What on earth was she doing letting Chase make love to her like this? She struggled to pull herself out of the deep well of sexual desire imprisoning her, but Chase was tracing light kisses between her breasts and caressing the flat smoothness of her stomach, his fingers drawing fiery patterns on her skin making it impossible for her to think rationally.

'Somer, touch me.' He moaned the plea against her skin, 'or are you deliberately trying to drive me mad?'

His teeth bit gently into her waist and she reacted instinctively, raking her nails in sensual protest against his spine, her own teeth finding the firm flesh on his shoulder. The smell and taste of him overwhelmed her, and without even being aware of it she was lost in a voyage of sensual discovery, her fingers stroking over his body, her lips following them, until Chase dragged her down into his arms and kissed her with savage impatience, his hands moulding her against him, his body arching into the cradle of her thighs and straining against her.

The knowledge that he wanted her physically was like heady wine, too tempting for Somer to resist. With an inarticulate murmur of pleasure, she pressed herself against his body, arching provocatively against him.

'You make me want you so much.' Chase kissed her breasts and the tender curve of her waist, kneeling over her as he bent to remove her briefs. Sudden shyness held her immobile, unable to look at Chase, her whole body tensed in expectation of his rejection. His hand covered the soft femininity he had just revealed, his voice raw with male need as he muttered thickly, 'I can feel your body telling me how much you want me, but I still want to hear you say it.' He bent towards her, stroking her parted lips with his tongue, teasing a small moan from them as he tormented her. 'Say it…'

Somer was too lost in her sensual daze to resist. Like someone listening to a hypnotist she murmured huskily, 'I want you…'

'Chase! I want you, Chase. Say it, Somer.'

'I want you, Chase,' she repeated obediently, tormented by the teasing arousing of his tongue.

'Now kiss me.'

Her lips parted willingly, brushing his. 'Not like that,' Chase protested thickly, 'like this.' His teeth tugged hungrily at her bottom lip, his tongue invading the moist sweetness beyond, until she responded with a mindless hunger that shuddered through her body. Her hand brushed against the soft barrier of his briefs, shocking her with the intimacy of what she was doing, reality piercing through the cloud of pleasure engulfing her. She wanted to draw back, but it was Chase who released her, muttering something under his breath.

This was it, Somer realised, tensing in mute resignation. He didn't want her. She shrank back from him closing her eyes, only to open them again seconds later to the glittering blaze of Chase's as he dragged her hand against his body and she realised that he had not been rejecting her but simply removing his briefs. The male heat of him was unfamiliar to her, as was his soft groan of pleasure as she touched him.

His body gleamed tautly male and golden in the fading rays of sunshine burning through the curtained windows. 'Touch me.' His voice stroked the words raggedly against her ear. 'You must know how much I want you to, or are you deliberately trying to torment me?'

She moved tentatively, tensing as she heard the hoarse groan he suppressed deep in his throat. 'It's no good, I can't wait any longer, I want you too much.' His hand slid between her thighs stroking them apart, his thumb describing erotic circles against her tense skin until she felt herself relax and shiver with pleasurable anticipation, and it was only when Chase covered his body with hers and she felt the hardness of his thighs pressing into her softness that Somer panicked. She was still a virgin! She couldn't endure the humiliation of Chase finding out; of him knowing that he had hurt her so deeply when he rejected her that she couldn't endure another man touching her.

'No...' She moaned her denial out loud, tensing her

body automatically and arching her spine against him in an effort to push him away.

'No?' A dark, ugly tide of colour swept up under Chase's skin, his voice bitterly incredulous. 'Oh no, you aren't playing that game with me. I won't be treated the way you've treated your other lovers.'

Other lovers? Somer arched frantically. Didn't he understand there hadn't been any other lovers? His fingers bit into her arms, holding her body prisoner, his thighs pinning her to the bed. 'Chase, please, you don't understand...'

'Oh, I understand all right,' he muttered furiously. 'You've had your fun and now you want to back out, leaving me as frustrated as hell. Well, not this time. This time you're not going to be allowed to back out...'

The driving male force of his body was something she couldn't fight or evade. She made a strangled protest deep in her throat as she felt the world explode in fiery pain, crying out incoherently.

'Somer.' Chase called her name roughly, disbelievingly, she recognised, willing herself not to cry out a second time. 'Just try to relax, I didn't...' He muttered something she couldn't catch and his body shuddered climactically against her, her own racked by tremors of pain and a dull empty ache that still clamoured for relief, even after Chase had withdrawn from her and was sitting on the edge of the bed with his back to her.

'Somer...'

'I don't want to talk about it.' Her voice was high-pitched with shame and agony.

'Why didn't you tell me you were still a virgin?'

'Why should I? Our marriage was supposed to be in name only, remember.'

She saw him wince, almost as though he had suffered a

physical blow. 'All right then,' he said evenly. 'I'll ask another question. *Why* are you still a virgin?'

'Why?' She fairly spat the word at him. 'You can ask me that after...'

'All right, you don't need to say anything more. I suppose I ought to have guessed when I saw you with Hollister this afternoon. You're still in love with him, aren't you?'

For a moment Somer was almost too astonished to answer. On the point of denying his allegation she hesitated. If she denied it Chase would want another answer to his question. As she looked at his taut back the truth hit her, almost numbing her thought processes. She had wanted *Chase* to make love to her. Not Andrew, not anyone else, just Chase. But that must mean that she loved him. Impossible, she told herself.

CHAPTER SEVEN

SOMER studied her reflection in the mirror applying her make-up with a decidedly shaky hand. If Chase had broadcast it through the medium of his television station he couldn't have made himself plainer, she reflected. The lovemaking which had started out, as far as he was concerned, as a form of punishment had ended with him repudiating her—finding her wanting, just as she had known he would. That blazing look of anger in his eyes before he had turned away from her, to sleep in the bedroom which had been hers, had told her how much he regretted his brief moment of weakness. He hadn't been in their suite when she woke up. She had sensed his absence in the thick, unnerving silence. She had ordered and then toyed with a breakfast she couldn't eat, her stomach nerves clenched in nervous dread, wondering where he was and when he would return.

As she replaced her mascara she heard the outer door open. Schooling her face not to betray her she picked up the lightweight jacket that matched her skirt and walked out of her bedroom. He was sitting in a chair, apparently absorbed in a paper, which he lowered as she walked towards him. His eyes skimmed her slender frame, resting enigmatically on her face. Hadn't the make-up she had applied so carefully hidden the faintly purple shadows beneath her eyes after all?

'I won't ask if you slept well,' he said grimly at last. '

imagine neither of us did that. Somer, I didn't realise when we married that...'

That she was still a virgin, he was going to say; and Somer couldn't bear it. She rushed into impulsive speech before he could finish, her eyes betraying her despair. 'Chase, please, I don't want to talk about it. I'm sorry you had to bear the burden of...of everything. I know how you must resent...what happened, but it's over now and I don't want to talk about it.'

'Over? Can you tell me that it won't happen again?' he taunted, his mouth bitter.

Had he expected her to stop him? Numbly she remembered telling him that their marriage was to be in name only, and his saying that he could stick to the rules, but doubting her ability to do so. Had his lovemaking been a test, a means of showing her that he was right and she was wrong?

'So, no answer, then I must take it that you can't.' Chase's coolly ironic voice interrupted her thoughts. 'Well then, I'll have to help you by removing at least some temptation out of the way. We're returning to London on the afternoon flight.' He saw her flinch and laughed harshly. 'If anyone asks, we'll say they needed me at the studio—it isn't entirely untrue. We're negotiating to buy an American series and the deal's causing a lot of problems.'

They were going home. Numbly Somer stared at him, the colour draining from her face. She wanted to laugh in hysterical disbelief. What temptation did he mean? That of sharing a suite with him? Did he think she had so little pride that she would throw herself at him, invade his privacy and beg for his lovemaking? A sob of self-disgust rose in her throat to be choked back, her chin lifting proudly. Well, if that's what he thought, she would have to show him otherwise. She would have to show that he was not going to get the opportunity to taunt her as cruelly as this again.

'No objections?' Chase taunted. 'No requests that we stay so that you can…renew old acquaintances?'

'What would be the point?' she asked coolly. 'If I object no doubt you would simply threaten to blackmail me again.'

'But I didn't need blackmail to have you in my bed, did I, Somer?' he asked with mocking cynicism.

She was already half way back into her own room, but she paused, turning to face him, trying to compose her features.

'What happened, Somer? Did you suddenly get tired of saving yourself for a man who married someone else?'

'I could ask you the same question,' Somer told him bitterly. A veil seemed to drop over his features, hardening them into a tight mask of rejection, and as Somer stepped into her own room, her head held high, she heard the door slam closed behind her. Leaning against it she gave way to the shivering tremors convulsing her, as she fought for self-control. The truce was well and truly over.

'WELL, Mrs McCleod, that seems to be everything.' Somer sat back on her heels surveying the packing cases and boxes littering the room, with a faint sight. Since her return from Jersey she had spent more time in her father's house than she had in Chase's. She used her father's imminent departure as her excuse and was cravenly glad to discover that Chase seemed to want her company as little as she wanted his. He worked long hours at the television studios often not returning until late in the evening. Most nights Somer ate alone, retiring to her small sitting-room to work on the various contracts she had in hand, before going to bed. If the cleaner Chase employed to take care of his house found it odd that newlyweds should sleep apart she managed to conceal it from Somer.

'You'll want to be getting home,' Mrs McCleod remarked. 'That husband of yours must be a very patient man. There's not many days you haven't spent round here since you came back from Jersey.'

'Chase understands that I want to make sure everything goes smoothly for Dad.'

'Aye well, only a couple more days now.'

'Yes,' Somer smiled uneasily. How on earth was she going to fill her days with her father gone? And worse, how on earth would she sleep at night without the physically hard labour of the last week or so to tire her out? Already there were nights when she simply lay sleepless, listening to every slight sound from Chase's room, remembering the feel of his hands against her skin; the wild pulsating torrent of pleasure his touch released in her body, and worst of all the unnerving moment of discovery when she realised that she loved him.

Tonight her father was taking them both out to dinner— a farewell celebration, if celebration was the right word, Somer thought despairingly.

They were dining at a new restaurant-cum-nightclub which they had recently opened, and she would much rather have not gone. For one thing she had nothing really suitable to wear. Sighing she got up off the floor and dusted down the knees of her jeans.

'I'd better be on my way.'

'Yes, you don't want to be late tonight. You're working far too hard,' Mrs McCleod added. 'You've lost weight since you got married—normally it's the other way round.'

Escaping before she could ask any difficult questions Somer drove slowly homewards.

The first thing she noticed when she reached the house

was Chase's car parked outside. As she slid out of her Mercedes her heart started to thud uncomfortably. It was unusual for Chase to be home so early, but surely no reason for her to start reacting like an adolescent carrying the burden of an impossible crush? But emotionally she was still an adolescent, she told herself bitterly.

None of her inner turmoil showed when she walked into the drawing-room. Chase was pouring himself a drink and looked up incuriously as she walked in.

'You're home early.' How banal and meaningless their conversation was, Somer thought wearily; they were two strangers forced to live in unwanted intimacy and the wear on her nerves made her wonder how on earth she was going to endure the twelve-month sentence. Of course it was worse for her. Since she couldn't even look at Chase without yearning to feel the hard warmth of his mouth possessing hers, and the heat of his body caressing hers with love and not merely physical desire, she had stopped looking directly at him, and instead addressed her comments to the middle distance, politely averting her eyes. But not before they had treacherously registered every single detail of his appearance, from the dark crispness of his hair to the business suit he was wearing. As she turned round he shrugged off his jacket, throwing it casually across one of the chairs. Beneath the fine silk of his shirt Somer could see the fluid play of his muscles. Every movement he made possessed a lean grace that made her ache with suppressed love. She wanted to go up to him and run her fingers along the contour of his spine; to have the right to slide her palms inside his shirt and feel the fierce pounding of his heart accelerate at her touch.

'Come back, you were miles away.' The harsh command broke into her dream. 'Stop thinking about him,' he continued coolly, 'it won't do any good.'

'What makes you think that...?'

His mouth curled sardonically. 'If you'd seen your own reflection you'd know why. You looked like a woman who was thinking of her lover.' He watched the colour come and go in her face and there was an unmistakable edge of anger to his voice as he said curtly, 'I'm home early because we're dining with your father, talking of which, isn't it time you went and got ready?'

He hadn't even offered her a drink, Somer thought bitterly as she closed the drawing-room door behind her. She didn't know what she had expected from their enforced marriage, but it hadn't been this emptiness...this hollow, lonely life with a husband in name only who was exactly that and nothing more.

The first thing she saw when she walked into her bedroom was the box on the bed. Frowning she walked over to it, noting the name of an exclusive Knightsbridge shop printed on the side. The shop was one she knew by repute only, being far too fashionable and expensive for her to patronise, but the name written on the lid was definitely her own. Curiously she removed it, searching through the swathes of tissue paper in which its contents were carefully packed.

The dress she eventually removed from the box made her catch her breath in startled disbelief. In a deeply dense sapphire blue the silk jersey was cut in a style she would never in a million years have chosen herself.

'Why don't you try it on?'

Somer spun round, staring white-faced at the communicating door that linked her room to Chase's. Ever since their arrival at the house she had kept it locked and retained the key. It had never occurred to her that Chase might have his own key, but evidently he had, and he had used it too.

'I didn't order it. There must be some mistake.' She turned away disdainfully, dropping the sapphire jersey in a pool on her bed.

'No mistake.' With half a dozen easy strides Chase reached the bed, retrieving the maltreated dress. 'Put it on, Somer, I want to see if it fits.'

'You bought it?'

'Don't look so shocked.' His mouth twisted with sardonic amusement. 'It is quite acceptable for a man to buy his wife clothes, indeed some women seem to believe it's a husband's primary function in life.'

'I won't wear it. I don't like it.'

'You will and I do,' Chase corrected inexorably.

'I don't need a new evening dress. I have plenty.'

'All of them as dull as ditchwater. They might have been suitable for the daughter of Sir Duncan MacDonald, but they aren't suitable for my wife.'

'Then I suggest you find yourself a new wife,' Somer bit out furiously, 'because I am not wearing that dress.'

'Oh yes, you are,' Chase told her softly, 'even if I have to dress you in it myself.'

Tears stung her eyes as she turned away from him. What was he trying to do? Turn her into the sort of glamorous model-girl type he preferred?

Without risking another look at him Somer picked up the dress, and still keeping her back to him, rummaged through her drawers for clean underwear. When she did turn round Chase was standing by the communicating door, arms folded across his chest, his stance one of relaxed determination. As she slammed her bathroom door behind her and locked it, Somer glared defeatedly at the sapphire jersey. Most women would be only too thrilled to change places with her; most women in her place loving Chase as she did would be doing everything they could to turn the situation to their advantage; using their enforced intimacy to promote an even greater intimacy, but she wasn't like that; she couldn't take the initiative; couldn't bear to allow Chase to so much as begin to suspect how she felt in case he rejected her again.

As she slid the silky fabric over her body she tried not to look at her reflection, but one wall of the bathroom was completely mirrored and seeing herself was unavoidable. The silk jersey clung seductively to her body, the long sleeves and high boat-shaped neck a demure contrast to the deeply plunging back. The straight skirt clung to her legs, the *diamanté* embroidery on the front of the dress flashing sparks of firelight with every movement she made.

As though he had been waiting for her, when she emerged from the bathroom, Chase came to lean against the now open communicating door, dressed only in a brief towelling robe, his hair still damp from his shower, the robe revealing a tormenting vee of flesh at his throat forcing Somer to battle against her urgent desire to go up to him and taste the cool male skin.

Indeed so total was her absorption in battling against her overpowering response to him that Somer was barely aware of Chase studying her until he said carelessly, 'It suits you, but you'll need these to wear with it.' He handed her a pair of silk stockings in the same deep sapphire as the dress, 'and these…'

Somer hadn't seen the small velvet box in his hand and she winced as he opened it and she caught the bright dazzle of diamonds.

'Come here.'

She stopped a yard away from him, tensing when his fingers curled round her wrist, tugging her closer.

'That's better.'

Somer just caught the deep blue and white fireflash of

diamonds and sapphires as he lifted one of a pair of sapphire and diamond-drop earrings from its bed of velvet.

While Somer stared, mesmerised at the brilliant stones, Chase swept back her hair and carefully fastened the earring in place.

'Chase, I...' Somer's throat ached with unshed tears, although quite why she would want to cry she couldn't understand. She stepped back awkwardly, anxious to put some space between them. This close to Chase's body, her senses were rioting tumultuously out of control.

'Thank you,' she said formally at last, when she felt she was in control of her breathing. 'Of course I'll return them to you when...when our marriage is over.'

For some reason her words angered Chase. A white line of temper circled his mouth, his eyes flat and hard. 'It's all right, Somer,' he told her harshly. 'You've already made it more than plain how little you want from me, but you must remember that a man has his pride. If I allowed you to go out wearing one of those dowdy garments that pass for your idea of an evening dress, I doubt if anyone would believe in the fiction of our marriage.'

When he saw her frown, he said harshly, 'A woman in love with her husband wants to dress to please him; to entice him, not to freeze him off,' he explained tersely. 'But then you aren't a woman, are you, Somer, you're a child still who puts her emotions and responses into cold storage because...'

On unsteady legs Somer bolted for her bathroom, just managing to suppress her tears until she got there. Dashing them away angrily with the back of her hand she forced herself to concentrate on the task of applying her make-up. So Chase thought she was dowdy, did he? Angrily she found a deep-blue eyeshadow to match her dress, applying it with quick sure strokes. A touch of blusher enhanced the pink flush along her cheek bones, mascara thickening and darkening her naturally long lashes. A deep-rose lip-gloss completed her preparations and Somer stared at her reflection for a few minutes, half surprised herself by the transformation. Gone was her normally cool and remote facade and in its place was the reflection of a woman she barely recognised, but who somehow looked warmer and, yes, much more physically responsive than the image she normally projected.

In order to show off her new earrings to their best advantage Somer piled her dark hair up in a soft cloud of curls. Finally ready she stepped back into her room and into a pair of delicate high-heeled shoes. Several tendrils of hair had escaped and she was just about to pin them up when Chase walked in. Somer caught her breath as their eyes met in her mirror.

'Leave them,' Chase ordered softly, pulling her fingers away from her hair. 'I like it as it is...'

'But it's so...untidy...'

'Not untidy, just feminine and approachable. As though we've spent the evening in bed and you had to get ready in a hurry.'

He watched her flush and laughed bitterly. 'I'm already well aware that the thought of my lovemaking fills you with distaste, but you'll have to forgive my small vanity in not wanting anyone else to be aware of it. I'll meet you downstairs in five minutes.'

He was gone before she could make any retort. Somehow it had never occurred to her that Chase could be vulnerable—somehow she had never equated such a human weakness with the man she had remembered him to be. But that man had never really existed, she reminded herself. He had been magnified out of all proportion by her own mind. The real Chase was weak and greedy; otherwise why would he have blackmailed her into this marriage? And yet despite everything she still loved him. That to Somer was the most unbelievable thing of all.

When she went downstairs he was pouring himself another drink. He smiled bitterly when he saw her check.

'No need to worry, my lovely wife, I'm not about to get drunk and disgrace you. What a pity Hollister can't see you now. How much he would regret his marriage to Judith, if he could, or is he already regretting it, Somer?'

'Everyone's entitled to one mistake.' Somer wasn't sure why she had said that. She had known instinctively before the words were uttered what Chase's reaction would be and she had been right.

'One mistake?' he sneered. 'Is that how you see it? Well, let's get one thing clear here and now, for just as long as you're married to me there'll be no pardon from you for that mistake, is that understood?'

'You may lie and cheat to get what you want out of life, Chase,' Somer retorted coldly, 'but I don't.'

For once she seemed to have the last word, although she couldn't help noticing that Chase's jade eyes glittered like obsidian as he watched her progress towards the door.

That evening was every bit as bad as Somer had anticipated it being, although she tried bravely to hide her feelings from her father. On reaching their destination they were shown to a discreet half-hidden table, the decor of the restaurant plainly geared for the privacy and delight of lovers rather than more prosaic diners.

While Somer sat in silent misery her father and Chase talked amicably; two men with interests in common and a shared level of intelligence who seemed to have forgotten that there was a third member of their trio.

'And what about you, Somer?' her father asked, suddenly seeming to remember that she was there. 'What are your plans for the future? Will you keep on with your computer programming or does Chase have other plans in mind?' Sir Duncan's eyes twinkled over his last comment and Somer knew he was thinking of the potential grand-chilren he was no doubt confident they would provide him with.

'I hope Somer will continue with her work for as long as she wishes,' Chase answered for her promptly, half sur-prising her with his vehemence. When Sir Duncan raised his eyebrows slightly he explained, 'I've seen far too many intelligent women become bored and frustrated wives, sub-limating their talents to those of their husbands, to want to see Somer doing the same thing, although I must admit I am fortunate in that she can work from home, but I never want her to feel that her own needs and desire for mental stimulation and fulfilment come second to mine.'

'Mmm, a rather unusual view,' Sir Duncan commented. 'In my day when a woman married, her husband, and then her children became her career.'

'Because they had very little choice,' Somer put in. 'Nowadays women do have a choice.'

'Some women,' Chase interrupted drily. 'There are women for whom nothing has changed—they have always had to work, when work is available, to supplement the family income, and I think, if asked, many of them would be more than happy to exchange the factory or sewing-shop floor for their own homes, and the opportunity to work now, for a large proportion of women, is not so much a choice as a necessity.'

'What do you say to that, Somer?' her father asked jo-vially, watching her teasingly.

'I think a lot of what Chase says is true,' she said slowly, picking her words with care. 'It must be heart-breaking for a woman with a small child to have to go out to work, when she would prefer not to, because her financial contribution to the household is needed. I think when people talk about the right of women to work; to share the mental stimulation of their men's lives, they forget that for both sexes there are many jobs which are dull and boring, simply a means of earning a living. Of course added to that there is always an added strain on a woman, torn between wanting to be with her children, and knowing that she can't be, even when she has chosen to work for non-financial reasons.'

'You'd want to be an "at-home" mother to your children then?' Chase asked her, watching her closely.

'Yes, I think I would. I should want to watch and enjoy their first few years at least and…'

'I think this conversation is becoming far too profound,' Sir Duncan broke in, 'and with no particular relevance at present, unless of course…?'

'No, I want Somer to myself for at least the first year of our marriage,' Chase answered, completely unembarrassed by her father's delicate probing. But then why should he be embarrassed, Somer asked herself bitterly. Chase knew there was no chance of them having a child. The admission was almost a physical ache inside her.

Just as they were finishing their meal the small band struck up and couples began to fill the dance floor. The music was unashamedly romantic and the sight of the closely entwined bodies of the dancers, lost in private worlds of their own, sharpened Somer's heartache.

'Why don't you two go and dance?' Sir Duncan suggested. 'Ignore her, Chase,' he chuckled, when Somer objected hurriedly to his remark. 'She's just being polite in pretending she'd prefer to stay here with me. I've seen the way she's been eyeing the dance floor for the last five minutes.'

Somer knew she was blushing hotly, and that her father no doubt thought her embarrassment sprang from her newly married status, but Chase, what did he think? She darted a quick glance at him as he stood up, his fingers cupping her elbow, guiding her through the semi-darkness with what would pass to outsiders at least as husbandly concern. Even in the half-light she could see the tight, held-in anger, tautening the skin over the bones of his face, and she flinched back automatically as he pulled her into his arms.

'Your father's watching us,' he grated against her temple. 'Do you want him to guess the truth?'

When she didn't reply, his hand moved along her spine, pressing her tense body into the hardness of his, forcing her along the length of his body, until she was aware of every unyielding muscle.

'We're only just married,' he murmured mockingly, 'and we're very much in love.' His fingers slid round the back of her neck, his thumb stroking the delicate skin behind her ear. Somer reacted as though she had been stung, fighting to suppress the immediate excited leap of her pulses, her eyes as brilliant as the sapphires suspended from her ears as she stared up to meet the mockery of Chase's green ones.

Sharp emotion trembled through her. She opened her mouth to beg Chase to stop tormenting her and then all coherent thoughts fled melting away beneath the warmly insistent pressure of Chase's mouth on hers. There wasn't time to take evasive action or resist. Her lips parted in mute submission, her senses responding to the seductive heat of his mouth with famished hunger. Somer forgot that they were in the middle of a dance floor; that her father was seated nearby; that Chase did not love her as she loved him; and gave herself up completely to his touch, loving the strength of hands that moulded her to his length, urging her to take pleasure from the intimate contact of their bodies.

It was only the harsh expletive that grazed across her skin as Chase released her mouth that brought her back down to earth.

'I told you resisting temptation wasn't going to be as easy as you thought, didn't I?' he mocked her as he set a small space between their bodies. For a moment Somer felt too bereft to dwell on his comment, her body ached for the warm pressure of his, her lips swollen and stinging, needing the pleasurable balm of his kiss, but the small movement she made towards him was checked as she realised what he had said.

Chase had known she wouldn't be able to resist him, despite her claim that she loved Andrew. Biting down hard on her quivering bottom lip she forced herself to meet his eyes. 'I'd like to go back to our table,' she told him quietly. 'I'm feeling rather tired.'

What could she say if he challenged her about her response to his kiss? Could she claim a mental aberration? Could she say she had forgotten who it was who held her in his arms?

Much to her relief they returned to their table in silence. Her father was waiting for them a reminiscent smile curving his lips. 'I used to take your mother dancing,' he told Somer. 'She was so light on her feet.' He pushed back his cuff and glanced at his watch. 'Well, I don't know about you two, but I'm ready for my bed.'

Somer didn't look at Chase, but to her relief he concurred with her father, rising smoothly to once again cup her elbow with proprietorial protection as they made their way outside.

Alone in her bedroom, Somer stood in front of her mirror as she removed her earrings and then cleansed her face, trying not to remember the smooth glide of Chase's fingers over the bare skin of her back. Shivering slightly she headed for the shower, trying not to think about how the evening would have ended if they were in love. Then Chase would not have left her in the hall, announcing that he had some work to do; they would have gone upstairs together, to a room that they shared; Chase would have slid the dark sapphire gown from her body without having to be asked, and she would... The shiver that ran through her had nothing to do with the temperature of the water.

Shaken by the wanton direction of her thoughts, Somer towelled herself briskly, and hurried through into her bedroom. For once the charming colour-scheme of peach and white failed to soothe her. Her bedroom was delightfully feminine and initially she had been pleased with it, but now it struck her very much as the room of a woman without a man to share it.

She wasn't asleep when she heard Chase come upstairs, but she buried her head beneath the bedclothes, not wanting to hear him moving about in the next room; not wanting the torment of knowing he was there and that only a wall separated them. Only a wall! She laughed silently to herself. It might as well be the Great Wall of China!

CHAPTER EIGHT

THE phone rang just as Somer stepped into the hall. It had
been a busy morning with her going to see her father off
at Heathrow and then having to rush back in order to complete a programme she had promised one of her old clients.

Chase had offered to go with her to the airport, but she
had curtly refused, knowing that the double emotional
strain of his presence and her father's departure would be
too much for her fragile composure. If she hadn't known
better she might have thought that for a moment she had
glimpsed pain in his eyes, before it was quickly shuttered
by a look of blank coldness.

She picked up the receiver, silencing the shrilling noise
of the telephone.

'Somer?'

Instinctively she tensed at the sound of Chase's voice,
forcing herself to relax as he demanded curtly, 'Somer, are
you still there?'

'I'm here, Chase. I've just got back from the airport.
Why are you ringing? Did you think I might have tried to
run out on our…agreement and gone with my father?'

'I left in rather a rush this morning.'

More from the tone of his voice than from his lack of
response to her gibe Somer guessed that he wasn't alone.
'I left some papers I need in my desk, I was wondering if
you could come round to the studio with them? I'd offer

to take you to lunch by way of recompense, but unfortunately I already have something on.'

He went on to tell Somer exactly where the papers were and rang off when she had agreed to take them to him. It only took a matter of seconds to find the envelope he had described. Somer glanced at her watch and then picked up the receiver, quickly punching out a number.

Her client was very understanding. 'I've still got a week or so in hand before I need the programme, Somer—I know how reliable you are with your time scales, but other people aren't so I always give myself some time in hand. It won't make any difference at all to us if we don't receive your work until next week. I must admit though that this isn't like you—what's causing the delay—a heavy date?'

He obviously hadn't heard about her marriage, and Somer explained quickly.

'My, my, that was all rather sudden, wasn't it? Somehow you don't strike me as the impetuous type. Seems like I was wrong, or did that new husband of yours just catch you at a weak moment?'

They chatted on for several minutes, with Somer deftly side-stepping an invitation to dine with her client and his wife.

'I see, still at the honeymoon stage are you?' he teased, not at all offended. 'Well, I can still remember what it's like—just about.'

How many more lies was this charade of a marriage to Chase going to force her to tell? Somer wondered bitterly as she started up her car. Chase was using her, callously and cold-bloodedly, and yet knowing that did nothing to destroy the love she felt for him. What kind of woman was she anyway? The kind who was only capable of loving and responding to one man, Somer thought sadly as she manoeuvred her car through the late-morning traffic. At least she no longer believed herself incapable of any sexual response, but then perhaps she had always known that and had hidden from the truth, knowing that to admit it was to admit her feelings for Chase; to admit that her almost instantaneous physical response to him sprang from a deeply intense love that her body had recognised long before her mind and heart were willing to acknowledge it.

The television studio was housed in an extremely elite office block, a uniformed commissionaire stepping forward as Somer entered the building and directing her towards the reception desk.

Beneath her smooth, faultlessly applied make-up Somer detected traces of curiosity—and something else—in the receptionist's glance as Somer gave her name. A frisson of uncertainty trickled down her spine. If she hadn't known that Chase was expecting her she might almost have believed the girl was flustered and somehow uncomfortable at her appearance. For the first time it occurred to Somer to wonder how Chase would deal with the effects of their marriage on the more personal side of his life. He had never made any pretence of living like a monk, and even discounting the publicity element, there had been a considerable amount of newspaper gossip about his 'affairs'. The most news-worthy had been with the actress Clancy Williams, Somer remembered, but their affair had ended when she had married someone else. That had been over a year ago, and although he had frequently been photographed with different, glamorous women, as far as Somer knew there was no one woman in his life at the present time. Apart of course from herself.

She grimaced faintly at the thought. She was hardly up to the standard of Chase's normal women, but then she had not been chosen for her looks, or for her sexual desirability. A fierce stabbing pain knifed through her body.

It took her several seconds to realise it for what it was. So this was jealousy; this surging, violent emotion that left her weak and vulnerable.

The receptionist had picked up her phone and had her back to Somer, murmuring something into it. There was a pause and she swung round to glance uncertainly at Somer. As she did so, whoever she was speaking to said in a voice perfectly audible to Somer, 'Are you sure she said Mrs Lorimer, Nan, only he's got La Clancy in with him at the moment staging a big reconciliation scene and I daren't go in and break it up.'

The receptionist swung back quickly, flushing slightly, and for her sake and for the sake of her own pride Somer pretended she had not heard.

Clancy Williams was with Chase? Had she developed some psychic power she hadn't known she possessed before, she wondered bitterly. Only seconds ago she had been remembering Chase's turbulent affair with the actress and now apparently she was here in the same building as Chase—in the same room as Chase. As far as she knew Clancy Williams was married. But what if she wasn't? What if she had left her husband? Would Chase regret marrying her?

It was pointless letting her thoughts torture her like this, Somer told herself, standing up and walking over to the receptionist who was replacing the receiver.

'Look,' she said pleasantly, 'my husband rang me and asked me to drop some papers round for him. If it isn't convenient for me to see him I'll just leave them with his secretary.'

Plainly relieved, the girl gave Somer directions to find Chase's office, walking with her to a small lift almost hidden by the display of greenery decorating the foyer. In-

stead of showing the floor numbers this one simply bore
the words 'Chief Executive's Suite'.

Once she had installed Somer safely inside it the receptionist flicked a button inside it and smiled reassuringly
'Turn right once you get out of the lift,' she instructed as
the doors started to close, 'Mr Lorimer's office is straight
ahead of you.'

The lift bore Somer upwards with stomach-lurching
speed, rocking gently as it came to a full stop. There was
a mirror inside it, which because of the harsh lighting
showed her a far less flattering reflection than she was used
to seeing. No doubt Chase found it an ego-bruising weapon
to use against those who came up to seek him out in his
lair, Somer thought, resisting the temptation to steal another glance at her make-up as the doors opened.

Following the receptionist's instructions she walked
down a short, thickly carpeted corridor which opened out
into an elegant foyer decorated with natural grass wallpa-
per and furnished with comfortable masculine-looking
leather chairs and a low table. Plants were banked up beneath the large window, adding a touch of greenery, although unlike the foyer walls downstairs which were
adorned with glossy prints of Television West's best
known personalities, these were completely bare.

An attractive brunette in her mid-twenties, immaculately
dressed and made up, smiled cautiously at her.

'Mrs Lorimer? Your husband did warn me to expect
you,' she said, 'but unfortunately he's rather tied up at the
moment.'

'Well, I've only called with some papers he wanted,'
Somer told her, 'perhaps if I were to leave them with you?'

'Well, yes, but if Mr Lorimer knows you're coming
in…' She bit her lip, plainly undecided about what to do.
It was obvious to Somer that she was reluctant to interrupt

Chase, but neither did she want to offend her, Somer could see, by denying her access to her husband.

Wanting to make things easy for her, and suffering from a cowardly lack of desire to see Chase with Clancy Williams, Somer handed over the papers she was holding and turned back towards the door, but just as she did so, the connecting door between his secretary's and his own office was opened by Chase, his hand resting lightly on the shoulder of a tall, elegant woman, whose eyes widened slightly as she saw Somer.

'Mr Lorimer…'

'Chase…'

His secretary and Clancy Williams both spoke at the same time, the secretary's hesitant, 'Your wife…' falling into the silence that followed.

'*This* is your wife, Chase?' Clancy Williams was plainly amused, although there was some hostility in the glance she directed at Somer. 'Good heavens, where on earth did you find her? Not your type at all, darling…is she?'

A cold finger touched Somer's spine. Chase was showing no inclination to leave Clancy Williams's side and come to hers. If anything the look he was giving the other woman was tenderly indulgent, while Somer had barely merited more than an irritated glance.

Well, no wonder he was looking at Clancy, Somer thought miserably. She was beautiful; and like any good actress knew how to project herself. Right now she was stage centre and loving every minute of it, Somer recognised.

'I couldn't believe it when I heard Chase had got married,' she told Somer pouting slightly, her eyes as hard as diamonds. Chase's secretary had diplomatically whisked herself out of the office, so there was no one there to witness her annihilation apart from Chase. 'I would have sent him a present—I saw some darling silk pyjamas in L.A. but then of course I know that Chase doesn't wear them.' Somer caught the brief smile that tugged at the corners of Chase's mouth and the look he and Clancy exchanged and rage and jealousy burned through her like a fireball; in that moment if she could have done so she would willingly have destroyed them both. Clancy Williams first, and Chase second—slowly and painfully.

'You must have caught him at a vulnerable moment,' Clancy told Somer unkindly. 'Or did you do it just to spite me, darling?' she asked Chase softly. 'Rather silly of you in view of the circumstances. Which reminds me, I have to go and see my solicitor tomorrow. You must come, with me, Chase, you know how hopeless I am about business matters.'

About as hopeless as a praying mantis at attracting food, Somer thought, raging with anger. How could Chase be taken in by that soft cooing voice and that mock helpless act? He was positively lapping it up, she thought viciously as Clancy added, 'I'm hoping my divorce won't take too long to come through, but it's such a traumatic ordeal, and then finding out that you're married.'

'We can still be…friends.'

'Friends?' She pouted again. 'Friendship wasn't exactly what I had in mind when I came to see you this morning, darling, but we can talk about that over lunch.'

So his business lunch was with Clancy Williams, Somer thought wretchedly. She might have known. All too vividly she could picture the two of them alone somewhere… It was pointless to imagine that Chase would even try to resist the sensual temptation of his one-time mistress.

'I'll just see Somer to the lift, Clancy,' she heard Chase murmur to his companion. 'Why don't you wait here for me?'

The look the actress gave her was all smug complacency, rubbing her head against Chase's shoulder like a purring cat.

Chase waited until he had closed the office door behind them and they were in the corridor to speak.

'Thanks for bringing the papers,' he said carelessly.

His casual attitude only added to Somer's sense of outrage.

'Yes, a pity I arrived just when I did,' she seethed, practically choking on the words. 'I hated to interrupt what was obviously a very emotional get-together.'

For a moment she almost thought she saw amused satisfaction gleaming in Chase's eyes, but it was banished very quickly; cool aloofness taking its place.

'Clancy and I are very old friends,' he told her curtly. 'She's flown in to London to talk to me about appearing in one of our new drama series.'

'And to tell you that she's getting divorced?' Try as she might Somer couldn't keep the bitterness out of her voice. 'Would you have married me, Chase, if you'd known that before our wedding?'

'I didn't know, did I?' He shrugged, avoiding the question. 'Besides there's no comparison between our relationship and mine and Clancy's...'

Somer went white with the pain of hearing him say it. 'No, of course not,' she choked, forcing back the tears threatening to ignominiously flood down her cheeks. 'I'm only your wife, while she's...'

'Clancy and I go back a long way,' Chase told her curtly, 'she's going through a very bad time at the moment. As a friend I owe it to her to help her as much as I can.'

There was something Somer had to know.

'Does she...does she know the truth about our marriage?' she asked woodenly, hating herself for asking the question and knowing that a humiliating flush of colour scorched her face.

Chase was watching her thoughtfully. 'I shan't say anything about it to her.' He smiled mockingly. 'I hardly think she'll want to discuss our marriage in any case, we have other things to talk about.'

And Somer could guess what they were. The look Clancy Williams had given her in the office had told her just how little she was prepared to tolerate Somer's presence in Chase's life. She wanted Chase, Somer acknowledged bitterly, and Chase probably wanted her. She couldn't ask him outright if he still loved the other woman because she couldn't bear to face the pain of his answer.

She walked into the lift without a backward glance, praying that he couldn't tell how upset she was. She knew she ought to return home and start work on her new programme, but somehow her mind refused to return to her work, but kept centring on Chase. She was becoming obsessed by him, she thought bitterly, still shivering from the effects of her blazing jealousy. She had never dreamed she could experience such powerful emotions and it frightened her to discover these unexpected depths to her own nature.

She was just pulling up outside the house when a taxi drew up from the opposite direction. The tall fair-haired man who alighted was instantly recognisable, and Somer locked her car, starting towards him.

'Andrew…'

He turned at the sound of her voice, his face alight with pleasure.

'Somer.'

'Andrew, what on earth are you doing here?' Somer was completely bewildered.

'Can't you guess?' His voice was huskily deep with

meaning. 'Oh God, Somer, I haven't been able to get you out of my mind. I had some leave owing to me, so I took it. I'm staying at our hotel in London—I told Judith I needed to get away for a while to sort myself out, but she wasn't deceived. Oh, my darling girl...'

'I'm not your darling girl—or your darling anything,' Somer told him tartly. 'Andrew...'

'Let's talk,' he pleaded. 'Please, Somer. I've come all this way just to see you...to talk to you. Have lunch with me.'

'How did you know our address?' Unwillingly Somer found herself propelled towards the taxi, where the driver still waited to be paid.

'From the hotel register. I haven't been able to get you out of my mind since you left,' Andrew told her thickly when they were inside the cab. 'Why did you leave like that?' he asked as the cab moved off.

'Chase had to come back,' Somer replied almost absently, still grappling with the discovery that Andrew had come to London to seek her out. She examined the thought and it left her completely untouched. If anything all she felt was a faint distaste that he could so easily abandon his wife and family...or was he lying to her? Was his visit to London simply a fortuitous opportunity to see if he could take up where they had left off all those years before? Andrew *was* an opportunist, she recognised, witness the manner in which he had bundled her into the taxi while she was still too bemused to protest. His treatment of her had left her with a mistrust of nearly all men, she realised as she coolly retreated to her corner of the moving taxi.

'Andrew, this is ridiculous,' she said at last. 'You're a married man.'

'And you're a married woman,' he countered huskily, 'but that needn't stop us finding happiness together. Oh, my darling Somer, if you only knew how often you've been in my thoughts...'

'Me, or my father's money?' Somer asked him drily. 'Really, Andrew,' she continued, 'you must think I'm still the same little fool I was at eighteen.'

'I know you are,' Andrew told her savagely, 'otherwise why would you have married a man like Lorimer? I know all about him, Somer; all about his women...beautiful women...'

'Whom I couldn't hope to compete with? Thank you, Andrew,' she said drily. Leaning forward she instructed the driver to take her back home. Andrew made as though to counter the instructions and then lapsed sulkily back in his corner. The journey was conducted in silence; an angry one on Andrew's part and mildly reflective on Somer's.

Poor Judith, she thought ironically when the cab came to a halt and she got out. Life couldn't be easy for her married to a man like Andrew. No doubt he made a career out of pursuing the more wealthy female guests. Her lips curled in a sardonic smile, quickly suppressed when Andrew climbed out of the cab to join her on the pavement.

'Somer.' He said her name urgently, grasping her arm.

'Andrew, we really don't have anything more to say to one another,' Somer began, breaking off when she saw Chase's familiar car coming down the road towards them. Why was Chase coming home? She glanced at her watch. Surely he couldn't have had lunch already? He never came home during the day. Conflicting emotions of pain and pleasure chased one another over her expressive face. As Chase brought his car to a standstill Andrew muttered something beneath his breath and then his arms came round her, his mouth closing determinedly on hers as he told her thickly, 'You might not want me now, Somer, but you wanted me once, and you owe me this.'

His kiss left her completely cold. Andrew released her
t her lack of response, and turned to step back into the
axi. Watching it draw away Somer knew that it was un-
ikely she would ever see him again. All she could feel
vas a vague sense of relief. She was just absorbing this
vhen Chase reached her.

'Somewhat less than gentlemanly, to leave you standing
n the pavement to face my husbandly wrath,' he drawled,
vatching her with an expression she couldn't name, her
ody tensing in shock as she witnessed the contrast be-
ween his smoothly drawling voice and the cold ice of his
yes. Explanations trembled on the tip of her tongue and
vere firmly suppressed. Why should she explain anything
o Chase? Especially in view of Clancy's obvious involve-
nent in his life.

'When did he arrive?' Chase demanded, staring after the
lisappearing taxi.

'Not long ago.' Somer averted her face. Chase's fingers
ightened painfully round her arm as he swung her round
o face him. 'And where were the pair of you planning to
go, before I turned up so unfortunately?'

On the point of denying his accusation Somer suddenly
changed her mind, a vivid picture of him with Clancy Wil-
iams reinforcing her decision.

'His hotel, I suppose,' Chase said grimly. 'Perhaps if
ou'd thought more about the instructions I gave you and
ess about your lover you'd be there with him. You
prought me the wrong papers,' he elucidated, as he hurried
ier towards the front door. 'That's why I came home.'

'And your meeting?'

'I cancelled it—so if you're thinking you can sneak back
o your lover the moment my back's turned—think again.'

'Andrew isn't my lover,' Somer blurted out the admission as Chase urged her into the hall.

'No,' he agreed softly. 'I've been wondering about that.' Somer was half way upstairs, and halted, alerted to something in his voice that warned her of a danger she could not see, but which she knew instinctively was there.

'Why wasn't he, Somer? After all, by your own admission you love him, and he obviously wants you. You could have gone to him any time during these last five years, but you didn't, did you? You didn't go to any man.'

He was right behind her on the stairs and Somer had no option but to continue upwards. She reached her bedroom and turned to close the door, only to find that Chase had followed her inside.

'Why, Somer?' he pressed. 'Why?'

'Why?' Somer trembled with the force of her emotions. 'How could I give myself to anyone, after the way you rejected me?' she cried out painfully. 'How could I give any man I loved what you had taught me was so completely worthless?' Once she had started it was impossible to stop, words, emotions she had dammed up for years spilled out until she forgot where she was and why she was there, and only knew that the pain inside her couldn't be suppressed any longer. 'I wanted you to make love to me,' she whispered painfully, 'but you rejected me. You'd made love to hundreds of women, but you rejected *me* ...'

'And because of *that* you remained a virgin?'

'Yes,' she whispered fiercely. 'How could I give to Andrew what you had shown me was so worthless?'

Somer felt as though she were in a dream—as though nothing that was happening was real. The explosive burst of temper which had precipitated her outburst had gone, leaving in its place an aching lethargy; a desire to be alone.'

'Somer, we have to talk.'

'What about?' she asked listlessly. 'We have nothing to talk about, Chase.'

'On the contrary,' he countered crisply, 'I should say we have a considerable amount to discuss.' There was a grimness about his mouth that she didn't recognise, an anger darkening his eyes that made him seem more alien than ever. 'If it's true that you couldn't allow anyone to touch you because of the past... Is it true, Somer? Is that why you were still a virgin—because of me?'

Beneath his tan his skin was oddly grey, a tension in his jaw that gave her the impression that he was holding some emotion in check so powerful that it made his muscles clench in protest. Was he angry because of what she had said?

'Yes,' she said huskily.

'And even though you love Hollister you never contemplated inviting him to become your lover?'

'And risk being rejected; being humiliated, the way you humiliated me? How could I give the man I love what you so obviously didn't want?' she asked wildly.

'Somer...'

'Don't touch me...don't come near me,' Somer cried almost hysterically as he made a move towards her. 'Just go...'

She heard her bedroom door closing softly behind her as she hugged slim arms round her shivering body. What on earth had possessed her to say those things? That they had sprung more from a desire to verbalise her pain on seeing Chase with someone else, rather than because she wanted him to believe she loved Andrew, she couldn't deny, but she had never meant to admit so much; to let him know how much his rejection had struck at her essential femininity, blunting and almost destroying it.

When she heard Chase's car start up outside she went

over to the window. Did he really glance up at her before he drove off, or was she just imagining it?

The afternoon dragged by and when Chase hadn't returned by eight o'clock Somer toyed unenthusiastically with her meal. At ten she went to bed, wondering if he was with Clancy Williams, and then deriding herself for wondering rather than knowing. Of course he would be. Chase wasn't a man to refuse any of the opportunities life presented him with, surely she knew that?

SHE WOKE UP feeling muzzy, not knowing what had disturbed her sleep. Outside it was still dark, her curtains moving in the light breeze through the open window. A small alien sound made her tense, her eyes searching the silent darkness. Something moved in the shadows. Still half asleep, thoughts of burglars made her go rigid with fear and then as he came towards her she recognised Chase's lithe frame and realised that the small sound which had awoken her had been the communicating door opening.

'Chase,' she said his name hesitantly, 'what are you doing here?' Her question died away as he bent towards her, pushing back the bed-covers. He was wearing a robe which he threw casually on to a chair before sliding his lean body into her bed.

'Chase…' she protested.

'Yes,' he said calmly, 'I heard you the first time. If you want a name for it you could say I am trying to put right a wrong I did five years ago.' His arm came round her before she could move, imprisoning her against the bed. 'I rejected you, you said, Somer, and because of that you were never able to give yourself freely to any other man.'

Somer sensed the tension in his body, and her first thought that he had come to taunt and mock her evaporated as her eyes adjusted to the darkness and she read the serious intent in his.

'Tonight if there's any rejecting, you'll be the one to do it,' he said softly.

She was trembling and Somer knew that he must be able to feel the betraying vibrations of her body.

'Chase, no,' she moaned softly, 'that was five years ago, and...'

'And no man has touched you ever since.'

'You have,' she reminded him indistinctly, 'when we were on Jersey.'

'Forget it, Somer,' Chase insisted. One arm, with all his weight behind it, still pressed her to the bed, his free hand cupping the side of her face. 'You and I are going back,' he said softly in the same mesmerising voice he had used earlier. 'Close your eyes, and forget everything else.'

'I can't.'

To Somer's sensitive ears her whispered admission confessed how much she would like to obey him, but Chase seemed unaware of it. His husky, 'Then perhaps this will help you,' seemed to reach her through a thick fog of indecision, and although she was fully aware of the downward descent of his mouth, she felt too languorous to avoid it. In some strange way it was almost as though Chase *had* managed to take her back in time, all her bitterness and torment forgotten as her lips parted hesitantly in obedience to the proximity of his, quivering slightly as though she were indeed that girl of eighteen again.

The pressure of Chase's mouth was warmly reassuring, gently explorative, slowly drawing her into a warm, womb-like place of safety, where her body knew instinctively that it could relax and reach out to explore the sensations his touch was invoking. The kiss deepened, and Somer followed the silent commands of Chase's mouth without question, sighing her acceptance from lips that parted instinctively.

Chase was lying full length against her, but she felt no alarm, no sense of fear, or excitement, merely one of acceptance. His arm ceased to imprison her body and he stroked the tumbled hair off her face as he released her from the captivity of his kiss.

Gradually, like the building of a tide, Somer became aware of the insidious drag of her senses. The brush of Chase's thumb against her lips was pleasurable and yet it made her ache to... She opened her mouth and touched the pad of his thumb experimentally with her tongue. His breathing quickened minutely and her heartbeat accelerated in response.

Slowly, leisurely Chase allowed his lips to drift across her skin. They lingered for intensely pleasurable seconds on the soft flesh beneath her ear and his tongue explored its delicate convolutions while she writhed helplessly in the grip of a bemusing response, her hands reaching out instinctively for the support of Chase's shoulders.

'We don't want this between us, do we?' Chase's fingers caught at the satin ribbons of her nightdress. Somer knew she ought to protest as he slid it from her, but his eyes burned darkly on her skin and she knew beyond all reason and rightness that she wanted that hungrily possessive male glance to devour every inch of her. As she felt his fingertips gently moving the gown away she protested weakly, 'Chase, this is wrong...'

'No,' he denied, letting his gaze rest on the twin peaks of her breasts. 'No, Somer,' he said huskily, 'it's right. It's what we both wanted all those years ago.'

'No...' Somer struggled against the sensuous response his words and touch invoked, trying to remember why it was she shouldn't feel like this; shouldn't be like this, with this man, but Chase was overruling her. Her skin felt scorched by his open study, her nipples tingling. When his hands cupped her breasts, holding them worshipfully, the last of her resistance melted away.

'Yes...' he muttered thickly, 'my Somer, yes. Tonight, I'm going to make love to you as I should have done five years ago. As I...' He groaned suddenly, leaning forward to kiss her hungrily, his hands freeing her breasts and gathering her up against him. The rough abrasion of his chest hair against her nipples made her ache with a wanton need to increase the sensual pressure, her body moving with unconscious provocation against his, until she was aware of the heat of him with every muscle.

Completely without check she gave herself up to his kiss, abandoning herself to the sweet storm of passion. Her hands moved eagerly over his body, shaping his shoulders, and sliding down his back to the indentation of his waist, and below to the narrow hardness of his hips and the flat muscular buttocks that clenched beneath her stroking fingers.

Gradually she became aware that both of them were breathing heavily; that their bodies were moistly fragrant and she wondered bemusedly if Chase found the softly feminine perfume of her skin as arousing as she found the heady masculinity of his.

Her lips, released from the captivity of his, quested along his throat, gradually growing more adventuresome as they met with no resistance. Indeed the moaned sounds of pleasure Chase muffled against her skin were an enticement as heady as newly fermented wine, and when Chase rolled over on to his back, taking her with him, Somer gasped at the pleasure of his lean body beneath her.

'Somer.' His thighs parted to cradle her in hard intimacy, and a suffocating heat seemed to burn through her body. She trembled violently and mistaking the cause of her reaction Chase muttered thickly, 'Somer, don't be afraid... I won't hurt you or reject you... You're so very beautiful, do you know that? So infinitely desirable... Let me show you how much. Let my body tell you all the things it's impossible to put into words.'

He moved and she felt the aroused throb of his body. He moaned as her fingers stroked uncertainly over his skin, pushing the upper half of her body slightly away from him. The hard contact with his thighs made Somer arch instinctively, her body seeking surcease from the dull ache building up inside her. Desire exploded inside her in waves of fierce heat. Throwing back her head Somer arched her back, unconsciously seeking completion of the union of their bodies. Her breasts filled Chase's hands, a dark tide of colour staining his skin, his eyes glittering feverishly, as he reached up towards her and caught one tender nipple gently between his teeth.

Somer cried out in surprised response, gladly allowing Chase to mould her thighs to the rhythm of his as his hands slid down to her hips. His tongue anointed the ripe crests of both breasts, and Somer was filled with a fierce elemental elation, responding to the wanton rip-tide that roared through her blood, gasping her pleasure at Chase's heated suckling of her breasts, conscious of the aroused heat of his body beneath hers and the harsh thud of his heart.

'Somer, sit up, I want to see all of you.' Chase's voice was so thick with arousal that Somer barely recognised it, but she had gone far beyond resisting now, or even remembering why she should resist. In obedience to his words, she let him push her into a kneeling position between his thighs. Sitting up so that they were almost breast to breast Chase's hands skimmed lightly over her body, etting off small tremors of response wherever they ouched.

His lips caressed her shoulder and then her breasts and Somer ached with the pain of loving him as she looked at he darkness of his head against her breast. His hands noved lower and she shook with reaction to his intimate nvasion of her body. She wanted to cry out in protest, but omehow the only sound she made was one that Chase eemed to construe as one of pleasure, because he made a hick murmur of response and his body trembled visibly as his mouth sought urgently for the turgid peak of her breast.

'Now,' Chase instructed thickly when he released her, 'I want *you* to look at *me*, I'm vulnerable too, Somer. Look at me,' he commanded softly, 'and you will see how much ny body desires you. You have the power to reject me if hat is what you want.'

He lay down watching her, and Somer felt her body shake in response to the feverish glitter in his eyes. She wanted to look away, but his body was a magnet drawing her bemused eyes.

Unconsciously Somer curled her fingers into her palms as she realised that Chase had spoken the truth when he said that he too was vulnerable. Slowly her fingers uncurled and she reached out to touch him, conscious of the aroused heat of his body beneath her finger tips. Her touch was one of discovery more than anything else, but Chase moaned and moved urgently against her, sending quivering bolts of lightning through her body overwhelming her with her need to know the fullness of his possession.

As though he knew her thoughts Chase said hoarsely, 'See how much you make me want you. Somer... Somer...'

Molten waves of heat flooded through her body as he

pulled her into his arms, kissing and caressing her body
into a hunger that matched his own.

'Now, Somer…now,' he muttered fiercely, his skin
damp against her. 'Take me inside you and make me feel
complete.'

In blind obedience Somer reacted to his words, marvel
ling at the shuddering vulnerability of his body as he
moaned thick exclamations of pleasure into her mouth and
throat, taking her with him on a powerful surge of pleasure
way beyond the barriers of human comprehension to a
place where merely spoken communication was com
pletely unnecessary and her yielding cries of fulfilment
were stolen from her tongue by the fierce heat of his
mouth.

SHE MUST HAVE fallen asleep in Chase's arms, Somer decided later, for the next thing she remembered was waking
up to find her body curled languorously against him, her
head buried against his chest and her legs still wantonly
entangled with Chase's.

A faint light filtered through the curtains warning that
morning was on the way. At first Somer felt completely
disorientated and then gradually she remembered, a deep
flush burning her skin as she did so.

'Now, can you still tell me that you feel rejected…undesirable…'

Chase was awake! Repressing a cowardly instinct to
play possum Somer tried to inch away from his body, but
he was holding her there with the arm he had curved round
her.

'Chase, you shouldn't have done it.'

'Why not?' he demanded bitterly, instantly releasing
her. 'Because I'm not Hollister? But I *am* the one who
rejected you, Somer, the one who refused to make love to

you and left you with a hang-up that has kept you a virgin ever since.'

'And now I'm supposed to be free?' Anger and pain shrilled her voice, as she realised fully why he had made love to her. As a recompense for the past. Surely an out-of-character reaction from a man who had had no compunction in using her.

'I suppose you expect me to feel grateful towards you as well,' she challenged, almost sobbing out the words in her chagrin and anguish. Out of a melee of thoughts only one was clear: Chase had made love to her out of pity...and some strange sort of guilt.

'Somer, I...'

'I'm sure Andrew will appreciate the expertise I've gained in your arms.'

The expression on his face changed, hardening.

'He won't get the opportunity to. We're leaving for Barnwell at the end of the week. The house isn't habitable at the moment—all the services are disconnected for one thing—but my sister's offered to put us up until we can move in.'

'Barnwell? You never said anything about us leaving London.' If Somer sounded shocked it was because she had never envisaged the undoubted intimacy of living with Chase in a small country village where she knew no one apart from himself and his family, but Chase chose to misinterpret her concern.

'It was never part of our bargain that marriage to me included easy access for Hollister,' he told her harshly. 'You come very highly recommended from your father as a good organiser and homemaker, so I might as well make use of your talent.'

'Meaning that it's the only one I have,' she challenged bitterly. To her surprise his lips twisted in the faintly mocking smile she was coming to know and he countered softly, 'Oh, I wouldn't say that... While it's true that your other...talents may not yet be honed to perfection, there's no doubt that the raw material's there.'

Thoroughly flustered Somer changed the subject. 'Tell me about Barnwell,' she demanded. 'When you say we can't move in straight away...'

'Oh, there's nothing structurally wrong with it,' Chase assured her. 'It's a soundly built house.' He yawned, suddenly stretching, reminding Somer of their intimacy—something she had almost forgotten in the heat of her anger against him. Dawn had broken fully now and as though he had read her mind Chase drawled softly, 'There's only two adequate reasons for waking up an hour earlier than you need to in the morning—the first is having an early business meeting, the second...' His glance lingered tauntingly on the full softness of her mouth and then moved downwards, gliding over her duvet-shrouded curves. Every muscle tensed, Somer stared back at him. Inwardly she was quivering with wild panic mingled with an aching feverish need which threatened to demolish her completely. She actually wanted him to make love to her again; to take her in his arms and caress her body, to...to tell her that he loved her.

Her heartbeats thudded almost to a standstill and then started up again; jerky staccato beats that told her of her anguish. Chase would never say those all-important words to her. Hadn't he told her why he was making love to her? Hadn't she seen him with her own eyes with Clancy Williams in his office?

'I must get up.' How breathlessly uncertain her voice sounded, almost as though she were hoping he would argue with her; plead with her to stay. Angry with herself she continued brittly, 'I've got some work to do... I should have done it yesterday, but I had to put it off to...'

'To take your papers to the studio,' she had been about to say, but Chase forestalled her, almost snarling, 'So that you could be with Hollister!'

'I had no idea Andrew was in London.'

'No?' He flung back the bedclothes, making no concessions towards any embarrassment she might feel at his nudity, Somer thought angrily, dragging her eyes away from the muscled perfection of his body. If they were really married, really lovers, she would be able to reach out and touch him; to coax him to stay with her and make love to her again.

She heard the bathroom door close behind Chase and tried to pull herself together. From the brief description he had given her she had no idea what to expect at Barnwell. It was true that she had organised her father's households for years, planning their decor, chivvying decorators and other craftsmen, but to do the same thing for a man who was virtually a stranger to her?

A stranger? Her own words mocked her. How could she describe a man who knew her as intimately as Chase did as a stranger? His heart and mind were locked and barred against her, and he was a stranger. She wanted to pull the bedclothes over her head and cry, but pride forbade her. When Chase returned from the bathroom he wasn't going to find her here in bed still, looking as though she were waiting for him.

'Somer, my dear, I hope I'm not ringing at a bad time?'

Somer recognised her new sister-in-law's voice almost immediately, and responded to her cheerful opening remarks, guessing that she was telephoning about their forthcoming stay.

'We can put you up quite easily at the moment, Dan and Chris, our eldest pair, are away in France on an exchange holiday, so we've plenty of space.'

'Chase says that Barnwell is structurally sound...'

'Oh yes, it is,' Helena agreed. 'But it has been very neglected. He's asked me to organise for all the services to be reconnected, and I've arranged for someone from the village to go in and give it a good clean up, but it is terribly old-fashioned; the house is Victorian and the kitchen hasn't been touched in the last fifty years at least. All the bedrooms still have their original fireplaces—but they're coming back into fashion now, and I don't suppose you'll be too worried about the size of the place—Chase was telling me what a good job you'd done on your father's London house. He said it was a proper home rather than a series of reception rooms. I can send you some photo-graphs of the interior, plus all the room sizes if that will help—of course you'll need to see the place for yourself, but I suspect once you have you're going to be kept busy flying between here and London—our small village and local market town won't be able to provide the fabrics and wallpapers I suspect you'll want. Still at least the place is large enough to house that football team Chase seems so keen on having.'

Talking to her sister-in-law was rather like being buf-feted by a rough autumn wind, pleasurably bracing but rather exhausting, Somer reflected when she eventually hung up. Against her will she felt drawn towards Chase's sister, and if the refurnishment of Barnwell proved any-thing like as time-consuming as Helena predicted it would at least be something to keep her mind occupied until her twelve-months' sentence expired. She would look upon the task as a job for which she had been employed, and per-haps with Chase busy at the studios and her involved at

Barnwell they need not see too much of one another at all; that way there would be no repetitions of last night.

Last night. She squeezed her eyelids tightly closed trying to blot out the memories; Chase looking at her almost tenderly… Chase touching her as though he wanted to give her pleasure, and then later as though he couldn't resist the feel of her skin beneath his fingers. His lovemaking had been all she had imagined all those years ago and more, eliciting from her a response that shattered her reserve, but it hadn't been lovemaking; it had been a self-imposed penance performed by a man she had never credited with the sensitivity to take on such a responsibility, never mind accomplish it with such acutely shattering delicacy.

But it was dangerous to delude herself that the man who had held her in his arms last night was the real Chase. He *was* a sensualist but she was far from being the only woman to find pleasure in his arms.

CHASE WAS HOME late that evening. Somer had eaten another solitary dinner and then worked on her programming. She was just flicking idly through a magazine when he walked in, trying to appear relaxed, while inwardly she was as tightly coiled as an over-wound spring.

The first thing she noticed was the alert, satisfied gleam in Chase's eyes, and for some reason it infuriated her.

'Sorry I'm so late,' he apologised. 'Something came up but I managed to get it sorted out over dinner.'

'Something not being Clancy by any chance I suppose?' Somer asked sweetly, astounded to hear herself sounding very much like a jealous wife. Chase seemed amused rather than annoyed by her comment.

'As a matter of fact I did have dinner with Clancy,' he

agreed, watching her as she strived to appear cool and uncaring. 'She's a very entertaining companion.'

'I'm sure she is,' Somer agreed waspishly, putting aside her magazine and standing up. 'I'm rather tired, I think I'll go to bed.

Chase paused in the act of removing his jacket, turning towards her as he tugged loose his tie and unfastened the top buttons of his shirt, stretching indolently.

For a long moment their eyes held and Somer was left in no doubt that he was remembering their lovemaking, and the gleam in his eyes was a satisfied very male one.

'I'm not tired because of that,' she bit out angrily, torturing her lower lip against her teeth as she saw the way he smiled.

'Because of what?' he asked lazily, not bothering to hide the amusement in his eyes.

'I've been working on a difficult programme today,' Somer told him, changing the subject. 'It's left me feeling rather drained—far too drained to sit here and unravel your innuendoes, Chase. Perhaps you shouldn't have rushed home quite so quickly,' she finished maliciously.

'Perhaps I shouldn't at that,' he agreed blandly, but Somer was quick to sense the chill in his voice. 'Did Helena ring you?'

'Yes. She's sending me some photographs and measurements of Barnwell.'

'Umm, well don't let her pressurise you into rushing— my sister tends to forget that the rest of the female population doesn't share her Amazonian tendencies.' The phone rang as he finished speaking and Somer reached automatically for it. She recognised the female voice asking for Chase almost immediately.

'It's for you.' She thrust the receiver towards him, almost shaking as she turned her head away.

'Well, it might be in the car,' she heard him say. 'I'll go and have a look.'

There was a brief silence while he listened and then as Somer turned towards him, his eyes fastened on her face and he drawled softly, 'No, no…if I find it I'll come round with it. You aren't interrupting anything that won't keep.'

'That was Clancy,' he told Somer unnecessarily when he had finished. 'She's lost one of her earrings and thinks it might be in the car.

Somer didn't comment. She felt too sick with jealousy to be able to do so.

It was very late when she heard him return, and she found she was holding her breath when she heard his bedroom door open. She could hear him moving about—showering in the bathroom which adjoined hers and then silence. Had he made love to Clancy? Had he touched her and caressed as he had touched *her* last night? she wondered, images of them together biting into her like acid. It was a long time before she eventually fell asleep and when she woke up it was gone ten and she was alone in the house.

CHAPTER NINE

IN THE end it was almost a relief to set out for Barnwell. The photographs and measurements had arrived—the rooms seemed large, and spacious, early Victorian as Helena had said. Until she had actually toured the house herself Somer didn't want to commit herself to any too fixed ideas, but in her mind's eye she could already envisage the high-ceilinged elegant rooms awash with soft pastels and chintz fabrics; perhaps some of the new Japanese-influenced ones...but she would have to consult Chase, after all he was the one who was going to live there, not her.

When she did so, Chase shrugged indifferently and said he would leave everything to her. 'I might as well get something from this marriage,' he taunted.

'You already are,' Somer shot back. 'Your uncle's fortune, and *you* were the one who wanted this marriage, Chase, not me. I had to be blackmailed into it—remember?'

'With photographs that you wanted me to take. Does Hollister know about them?'

'No!'

Her shocked recoil made Chase laugh grimly. 'No, somehow I thought he might not. Does he know that we have been lovers? Does he know why you have this hang-up about not making love?'

She was saved from answering by the insistent ring of

the telephone, and escaped upstairs to continue with her packing.

Chase was caught up in difficult negotiations over the American series—or at least that was what he told her and so the burden of preparing for their move fell on Somer. She had asked him what he intended to do about the London house and had been disconcerted when he replied that he would keep it on and live in it himself during the week.

'Try not to look so relieved,' he told her drily, misinterpreting her reaction. 'I had thought...but I hadn't realised then...'

'That my hang-up prevented me from becoming a casual bed partner as well as a means of obtaining your inheritance,' Somer said scornfully.

'Somer, are you all right?' His sharp query broke through her painful thoughts. 'You went quite pale,' he said watching her. 'Are you all right?'

'Of course,' she responded crisply, adding calmly, 'I had a letter from my father this morning. He seems to be settling in well.'

'Don't worry,' Chase broke in sardonically. 'If you want to remain a princess in her ivory tower, yearning over her lost love, I'm not going to stop you. I know better now than to cast myself as Sleeping Beauty's prince, although you did respond to me,' he added, making it plain what he alluded to.

Somer hated the painful flush that scorched her skin. 'You know why...'

'Because you hadn't been able to get over my supposed rejection of you five years ago? Yes, I know why,' Chase agreed, and Somer wondered if her imagination was playing tricks on her when she heard what she could have sworn was bleak bitterness in his voice.

'I've got to go now, if I want to finish early tomorrow.

We'll drive down to Barnwell late morning. Do you need any help with anything?'

'No. I'm all ready. There's just your things to pack.'

'I'll do that myself,' Chase cut in abruptly. 'I've got to go now.'

'NOT MUCH further now.'

It was the first comment Chase had made since they left the motorway behind half an hour ago. The comfort of his car had lulled Somer almost to sleep, and she pulled slightly against the restriction of her seat belt, noticing for the first time the loveliness of the countryside. Gently rolling hills, chequered in greens and golds, stretched out around them. The narrow road they were driving down was bordered with fields, clumps of trees interspersing the hedges.

'There's Barnwell.'

Chase stopped the car on the crest of a small hill. Below them Somer could see a cluster of houses which Chase told her was the village. Dotted round the periphery were half a dozen or so large dwellings, and then as she followed the direction Chase was indicating Somer saw Barnwell for the first time.

Victorian it most certainly was, but where she had expected austere patriarchal Victorian she saw a house mellowed by age, in warm buttermilk cream, ivy and soft yellow roses smothering the walls.

'It's lovely.'

She couldn't keep the surprise out of her voice.

'Yes.' Chase's agreement was soft. 'I've always had a special feeling about the place—perhaps because it was the only permanent home Helena and I knew as children. It's very special to me.' The quiet admission brought the betraying sting of tears to her eyes. Against her will she was picturing Chase as a child, missing his parents and clinging to the security of a house that exuded it. Stop making excuses for him, she warned herself when she found herself thinking that it was understandable that he would want to hold on to such an inheritance.

'Could…could we go and see it now?'

Somer was as surprised to hear herself voicing the request as Chase seemed to hear it. The plan had been that they would go straight to Helena's and yet something in Chase's expression as he looked down on the house tugged at her heart.

Without saying anything he set the car in motion, but Somer wasn't surprised when they drove in through the open gate and down a rhododendron-lined drive that led to the house.

'It's so tranquil.' For some reason Somer found herself whispering.

'Not when Helena is round her with her brood it isn't,' Chase drawled drily, 'and I suppose she and I were just as bad when we were kids. Our uncle was my father's uncle really, which makes it all the more remarkable that he was willing to take on the responsibility for it. He had been a teacher, and he had a way of imparting information that was so gentle that you didn't even realise you were being taught.'

There was so much love and affection in his voice that Somer glanced at him in surprise. Where was the anger and resentment she had expected? Chase hadn't been pleased about the strings his uncle had tied on to his inheritance and yet he was talking about him so caringly.

'He was the one who first started me on photography,' he continued. 'It was one of his hobbies. Our parents were still alive in those days, but we always used to spend some of the school holidays with him. He was…someone I feel privileged to have known. He enriched my life and I…'

He broke off and Somer whispered, unable to stop herself, 'I thought you hated him. The way he's tied up your inheritance…'

Chase had his back to her, and he shrugged powerful shoulders. 'He was very old when he died, old people do odd things. Do you want to go inside?'

She did want to, but she sensed that Chase's mood was broken. Painfully she realised that he probably wanted to come here alone, and that she was an intruder in his memories of the past.

'No… I'll leave it until later. Helena will probably be wondering where we are.'

Helena's house was on the other side of the village. Their house, although by no means as large as Barnwell, was comfortably substantial. The younger twins, Ben and Robin, came rushing out to welcome them, followed at a more leisurely pace by a fatly placid golden retriever, plumy tail beating the grass as they emerged from the car.

'Mum's burned the lunch,' Ben offered laconically. 'It was going to be lasagne, but now it's salad.'

'Benjamin Bailey, you traitor,' Helena scolded, emerging from the house in time to catch his comment. 'If you hadn't told them they would never have known.'

'Yes, they would,' Robin supported his twin. ''Cos you can smell something burning and salad doesn't burn.'

'I think I must be the world's worst cook,' Helena groaned when she had greeted them. 'Thank heavens for fast food, that's all I can say. The trouble is I start off with the best of intentions and then somehow I get distracted… Excuse the chaos,' she apologised as she led them in to a large but cluttered hall. 'Robin decided to start stripping down his bike this morning. Unfortunately when I agreed that it was a good idea, I didn't realise the exact location he had in mind.'

'But you said we weren't to go outside and get dirty,' Robin cut in in aggrieved accents. 'How long are you staying?' He fixed Somer with a piercing stare, but she liked children.

'It just depends...'

'Umm...well, I hope we don't have to stay clean all the time you're here. Mum said that you wouldn't like noisy, dirty boys...'

'Oh, I don't know,' Somer valiantly tried to hide a grin.

'See, I told you,' Ben threw in triumphantly. 'I mean she is married to Uncle Chase, so she must like him and he gets dirty...very dirty, last time he was here and he tried to oil my bike...'

'You mean when you left that can of oil right where I'd knock it over,' Chase interrupted wrathfully. 'Helena, can't you control these brats?'

'Hush, wait until you've got some of your own, then ask me that.'

'Are you going to have a baby?' Robin glanced with some interest at Somer. 'Mrs Hargreaves is but she's very fat...huge...like when Suzy had her last litter...'

'Robin,' Helena cut in hastily, 'that will be enough. Go upstairs both of you and wash your hands for lunch. No, on second thoughts you'd better wash down here, where I can keep an eye on you. You wouldn't believe how filthy two boys who I swear do no more than look at a bar of soap can make a bathroom,' she told Somer. 'Which reminds me, I'd better show you up to your room.'

Deftly skirting the dismantled bicycle, Somer followed her upstairs, leaving Chase still talking to the boys. This was what she had missed as a child, she thought enviously, this was what she wanted for her children. Almost without

conscious thought she could picture them, boys with
Chase's dark hair, relentlessly energetic, girls with soft
dark curls and dimples, who would probably be outrageous
tomboys, turning into *femmes fatales* overnight, twisting
Chase round their little finger....

'This is the guest-room.' Helena pushed open a door, to
reveal a pretty room decorated in blues and creams, 'and
the bathroom's through here.' She opened another door.
'We were going to put you in the twins' room because it
is larger, but then John reminded me that you're still very
newly married and the twins have single beds.' She
grinned. 'When we first bought them they used them as
trampolines, and I shudder to think what might happen if
you and Chase...' She broke off when Somer coloured and
raised her eyebrows. 'You're married to my brother and
you can still do that,' she marvelled. 'I don't believe it.'
The telephone started to ring downstairs.

'Oh, hell, I'd better go and answer it. Robin and Ben
are the world's worst for forgetting messages. I'll send
Chase up with your cases, and then we'd better have lunch
before the kids start complaining that I'm starving them.'

When she had gone Somer walked over to the double
bed, absently smoothing the quilt. The bedroom window
overlooked a large back garden sheltered by trees. Downstairs she could hear the deep rumble of Chase's voice
interspersed by the lighter ones of the twins. A double bed;
somehow she had never envisaged that she and Chase
would even be sharing a room, never mind a bed, but what
on earth could she do? Helena would be sure to find it odd
if they asked for separate rooms, and suddenly, traitorously
she wanted to hang on to the illusion that they were a
newly and idyllically married couple, who couldn't bear
to be apart from one another. Besides they wouldn't be
here for very long. Chase was still involved with the ne-

gotiations for the new American series, and had to be back
in London for meetings later in the week. He had manoeuvred her into their marriage. He wanted her services as
an interior designer more than he wanted her as a wife.

She heard him coming upstairs and remained where she
was studying the view.

He brought in their cases and then came to join her. 'No
comment?' he said raising his eyebrows.

Somer shrugged. 'Helena doesn't know the true circumstances of our marriage. I didn't want to upset her.'

'Of course,' Chase agreed sardonically, 'I should have
realised. After all it could hardly be that you would want
to share a bed with me, could it?'

He was gone before she could make any comment, leaving her to puzzle over the bitterness underlying his words.
Why should he feel bitter? *He* didn't want her love.

Lunch was muddled, almost a breathless meal, with constant interruptions from the telephone, interspersed with
Helena's lectures on manners to the twins. After lunch
Chase suggested that they go to Barnwell. The twins clamoured to go with them, and although Chase demurred,
Somer could tell that he was quite pleased when she overruled him.

Installed in Chase's car they were full of enthusiasm for
its electrical gadgetry.

'Dad's car doesn't have electric windows.'

'No? You do surprise me,' Chase commented sardonically, exchanging looks with Somer when the back windows had been raised and lowered for the umpteenth time.
'I can begin to see why some parents are so keen on rear
seat belts. Physically restraining these two gets more attractive by the second.'

The twins set off to explore the grounds while Somer
and Chase went into the house. It smelled dry and sound,

although as Helena had warned the decor was exceedingly
dingy. They started with the cellars where Chase told Somer he had once had his dark room. There was nostalgia
in the way he looked round the empty spaces that told
Somer that he was remembering those boyhood days.

The kitchen was every bit as dreadful as Helena had
warned although Somer itched to see what could be done
to restore the old range. The room was large enough to be
turned into a proper family kitchen, and she had fallen in
love with the tiled floor.

The drawing-room had windows on three sides and was
filled with sunshine, soft butter yellows and blues in this
room, Somer thought, visualising it. The sitting-room was
painted in dingy cream, the woodwork dark brown, but
there were glass-fronted cupboards built in at either side
of the marble fireplace, just built to hide the clutter of
children's toys, and the room was easily large enough for
a squashy settee and all the other paraphernalia of family
living. On the other side of the hall was the dining-room,
large and gloomy, and another good-sized room that Chase
told her had been his uncle's study, and which she could
easily visualise decorated in rich masculine colours, a re-
treat for Chase to escape to when the rowdiness of family
life threatened to get too much for him.

'I suppose it takes a good deal of imagination to see
how it could be,' he commented drily when they moved
upstairs.

Her problem was that she could see how it could be
done, all too easily, Somer reflected, and not only was she
mentally refurbishing the house, she was also equipping it
with a family—their family!

There were six good-sized bedrooms and a huge and
antiquated bathroom, plus a couple of smaller box-rooms
which could be turned into additional bathrooms. Only

three of the bedrooms were furnished—like the downstairs rooms with oddments of furniture.

'Think you can make something of it?' Chase asked laconically as they headed back downstairs. Somer had just been picturing the two of them sharing the king-size bed the master bedroom called for.

'Depending on the sort of budget you've got in mind, yes.'

Chase named a figure which made Somer raise her eyebrows a little.

'I came into some of my inheritance when we got married,' he told her by way of explanation. 'So you needn't stint. This house means a lot to me.'

'But you can't make your home here and work in London,' Somer pointed out.

'Maybe not at the moment, but I'm thinking of taking a less active role in T.V. West, acting more on a consultancy basis. I've got one or two other irons in the fire, and with my inheritance. This is a family house and it cries out to be lived in.'

'But you haven't got a family...'

His eyebrows rose. 'I've got a wife though, and that's generally reckoned to be a good beginning.'

The twins came bursting in before Somer could respond, and the four of them explored the large garden together. Some maintenance work had been done on it, and Chase showed her where he thought a conservatory could be built. 'We could have a swimming-pool as well,' he added. 'There's plenty of space, and I can't see why we wouldn't get planning permission.'

'A swimming-pool?' Two pairs of eyes rounded. 'Oh, boy....'

When they got back John Bailey had returned, and the appetising smells emerging from the kitchen suggested that

Helena's culinary talents weren't as lacking as she had suggested.

'I'm afraid we'll be having dinner unfashionably early,' she apologised to Somer. 'I hope you don't mind. It won't be the sophisticated affair you're used to.'

If only she knew. Somer thought about the solitary dinners she had consumed recently and suppressed a small sigh.

The chicken casserole Helena had prepared was mouth-wateringly tasty. Somer drank more than her usual single glass of wine, finding herself relaxing and responding to John's teasing bantering, as well as laughing at the twins' seemingly inexhaustible supply of jokes.

Afterwards she found herself being told to sit down and enjoy her coffee.

'We will wash up,' Chase told John, steering his sister into an empty chair opposite Somer's.

Although Helena chatted entertainingly, Somer was dismayed to find her eyelids dropping.

'I'm sorry, I seem to be falling asleep,' she apologised guiltily, wondering what on earth Helena must think of her.

'Don't worry about it, I always feel like that when I've been travelling. And when I'm pregnant,' she added after a thoughtful pause. 'Why don't you go up? I'll tell Chase when they've finished in the kitchen. He probably dragged you miles round Barnwell this afternoon—really it's no wonder you're tired.'

It was almost too much of an effort to get ready for bed. Somer opened her case and removed her nightdress and toilet bag. Chase's case was on the chair by the bed. Ought she to unpack for him?

Stifling a yawn she headed for the bathroom. It was bliss to sink down into the warm scented water, and she gave herself up to the luxury of it. Tomorrow she would start making definite plans for the house. She already had a good idea of what she wanted to do...

Lost in her thought she barely heard the click of the bathroom door as it opened.

'Not going to sleep in there, are you?' Chase drawled, his eyes skimming the mother-of-pearl sheen the water imparted to her skin.

Somer tensed, fighting off the urge to cover her nude body. 'What are you doing in here?'

It was a stupid thing to say, and Chase's wry grimace told her he shared her opinion.

'It is my room too,' he pointed out, 'and I'm tired as well, so unless you want to share your bath with me, I suggest you climb out before I join you!' As he spoke he pulled a soft fluffy towel off the rail and held it out to her. Somer wanted to ask him to leave, but in the circumstances it seemed a childish gesture. He had already seen all of her there was to see, she reminded herself, and seemed less than affected by it. She stood up slowly and stepped out of the bath, reaching for the towel and stepping past him.

'I won't be used as a substitute for Clancy Williams, Chase,' she told him shakily, knowing as she spoke that the words were more to bolster up her own faltering determination than because she thought he might actually do so.

'You couldn't be,' he assured her sardonically, 'Clancy is an experienced woman, not a cowering, frightened child.'

Painful colour stung Somer's cheeks as she retreated from the room. With half a dozen or so carelessly chosen words Chase had reminded her exactly how inadequate she was.

She was lying tensely awake when he eventually came to bed. She lay, waiting for him to unfasten his case, and then turned over when he didn't. He threw his robe casually over the back of a chair and then paused.

Somer swallowed. 'Aren't you…haven't you brought anything to wear?' she asked feebly.

'Don't worry, Somer,' he drawled, 'you're perfectly safe. Go to sleep and dream of Hollister if that's what turns you on. The only thing is,' he continued unforgivably as he slid into the bed beside her, 'that *he* doesn't seem to be able to do so, does he?'

THEY SPENT four days with Helena and John. Each night Somer went to bed, praying that a miracle might occur and Chase would turn to her in the night and take her in his arms, murmuring words of love, but of course, he didn't.

When she tried to talk to him about Barnwell, he shrugged and said, 'I'm quite happy to leave all that to you.'

'But I'll need to come up to London to order all the fabrics, and organise the decoration,' Somer persisted.

'Then come back with me tomorrow.'

'I thought you wanted me to stay down here,' Somer reminded him bitterly, 'away from the temptation of Andrew.'

'Maybe I can't resist the temptation of having you in my bed,' Chase responded.

Somer bit down hard on her bottom lip. They both knew how easily he could avoid that particular temptation—unlike her. Only this morning she had woken up to find she had curled closer to him in her sleep, her body instinctively seeking out the heat and security of him. Luckily she had woken first—which was quite unusual, Chase was normally the first to wake up—and she had managed to move away before he realised what she had done.

In the end she and Chase travelled back to London together. She wasn't looking forward to going back to her lonely bed, Somer admitted when they went inside the house. Chase walked straight into his study and within minutes Somer heard him talking on the phone. She herself had a large pile of correspondence that needed to be dealt with, and Chase was still on the phone a couple of hours later when she set out for Osborne & Little's showrooms. She knew they would be able to supply her with the papers and fabrics she wanted, and it made sense to use one supplier where she could.

She found them every bit as helpful as she had expected, and came away several hours later feeling that a great deal had been accomplished. She was particularly pleased with the soft yellow Japanese-inspired fabric they had opted for for the drawing-room, and they had promised that the soft blue-grey colour that featured in the fabric could be matched to the plain carpet she wanted for the drawing-room floor.

The dining-room was going to have ecru silk wall-hangings—to show off the rich oriental carpet she had in mind for the floor. The sitting-room and Chase's study still had to be finalised, but she was pleased with the progress she had made.

Pleasurably tired, she let herself into the house. There was no sign of Chase, and it was the cleaner's day off. In the kitchen Somer made herself an omelette which she carried through and ate watching television. In the middle of the play she was watching there was a newsflash. Her plate crashed down on to the carpet as she listened disbelievingly. There had been an uprising in Qu'hoor—as yet very few details were known, but it *was* known that the British Embassy had been stormed—as had the royal palace.

Her father! Shakily Somer rushed to the phone, and looked up the number of the Foreign Office.

Or course there was no reply, but someone must know what was going on; someone must be able to tell her. For a moment she entertained crazy notions of rushing round to No 10 and demanding to know what had happened to her father, and quickly suppressed them.

Chase! If only Chase were here! Quickly she dialled the number of the studios, and asked for him, anticipating a negative response. The telephone clicked and she sighed, her thoughts a panicky whirl.

'Somer?'

'Chase!' Her voice went weak with relief. Half crying, she told him about the news flash. 'Chase, my father...'

'I'll see what I can find out,' he promised. 'Try not to panic.' The phone rang almost the moment Somer put it down, and she snatched up the receiver, but it was only Helena calling to ask anxiously about Somer's father.

It was the first of a dozen or more similar calls, and Somer was near to screaming point when she heard the front door open and then slam closed.

'Somer?' Her heartbeats quickened as she heard Chase's voice. His hair was ruffled, and he looked tired. 'I came back as quickly as I could. Have you heard anything?'

'Nothing.' She tried to sound calm, but her voice quivered. More than anything else she longed to go to Chase and be enfolded in his arms, to share with him her pain, but she didn't have that right.

Chase picked up the telephone receiver and punched some numbers into it. 'Why don't you go to bed?' he suggested, throwing the comment at her over his shoulder. 'I'm going to make some phone calls. Use my contacts to find out what I can, but it could take hours with a nil result. You look exhausted.'

'So do you…and besides I couldn't sleep.'

The hours that followed had a nightmare quality, telephone calls punctuated by brief silences. Each time the phone rang her heartbeat accelerated, only to fade when Chase's enquiries elicited no response.

'The problem is that there's just no information coming out of Qu'hoor,' Chase told her. 'Even the FO doesn't know anything apart from the fact that there *is* an uprising.'

It hadn't surprised Somer that Chase had known immediately whom to contact. His efficiency comforted her, but not as much as his tenderness would have done. At two o'clock he said firmly, 'You're going to bed. I still have one or two contacts I haven't tried—some of the American stations have stringers in the Middle Eastern countries, they might know something, but there's no point in you staying up.'

'I'd never sleep.'

'You will if you drink this.' Chase poured her a large measure of brandy and then stood over her as she drank the fiery liquid.

Knowing that Chase was right and that she couldn't do anything to help, and yet wanting to stay, she went upstairs reluctantly, quickly undressing and showering.

Two hours later she was still restlessly awake, her ears stretched for the ring of the phone. Knowing that sleep was impossible she slid out of bed, reaching for her robe, and finding instead that her fingers had curled round the soft towelling of Chase's. It carried faint traces of his body scent and she found herself sliding her arms into it, craving the comfort of it.

When she got downstairs Chase was seated by the

phone. He had unfastened his shirt, and his face was etched with exhaustion.

The phone rang and he reached for it, his movements lacking his normally smooth coordination. As he looked up he saw Somer and tensed, and then his entire concentration was fixed on whoever he was talking to, staccato questions bitten out and answers received, while Somer clung unsteadily to the back of a chair.

'Don't look like that,' he said wearily when he had finished. 'Your father's alive and well. Apparently he was out of the capital when the coup took place. He had been invited to visit one of the minor princes, and decided to accept the invitation at the last moment. He was there when news reached them of the coup and he's now safe in Saudi, but because of the panic it's taken some time to get the news through. Hey,' he said softly when he saw the slow tears gathering in her eyes and sliding down her cheeks. 'Hey, come on, it's all right... Somer, it's all right.'

Somehow she was in his arms, where she had longed to be and they had closed around her. She started to shake as she breathed the musky scent of his skin, going boneless as relief and pleasure mingled in a dangerously heady aphrodisiac.

'I can't believe that he's safe. He's all I've got...'

'Apart from me.'

She knew that Chase was only trying to lighten her intensely emotional mood, but her heart started to hammer in response to his soft comment and she wanted more than anything else in the world to stay where she was.

'You must be tired.' She whispered the words into his throat.

'Umm...and in need of a shower, but that's going to be difficult...'

'It is?'

Both of them were talking in husky whispers, although there was no one to overhear them. The phone rang again and Chase picked it up. It was the Foreign Office confirmation of the news about her father. Chase kept her within the circle of his arm while he spoke and then left the receiver off the hook.

'Let anyone else who wants to find out what's happened, find out for themselves. I'm going to have to repossess my robe if I'm going to have a shower—you don't like me walking about in the nude—remember? Although it seems that one of us... You aren't wearing anything underneath it, are you?'

She wasn't. She had felt too hot to sleep after the brandy Chase had given her, and had discarded her nightdress.

'Come on...we might as well try to get some sleep for what's left of the night.' Chase bent and picked her up in his arms. 'You look ready to fall asleep on your feet.'

Upstairs he pulled back the covers of her bed, before placing her on it. Somer watched him disappear in the direction of the communicating door with an aching heart. She was still wearing his robe and she cuddled into it, drawing comfort from its warmth around her. She was practically asleep when Chase came back, a towel wrapped round his hips, his body gleaming soft gold in the light from his room, the dark hair on his chest, still slick with water.

'I've come back for my robe.'

'No.' Somer clutched protestingly at the soft fabric, uttering the denial without thinking. 'No, don't take it away from me. It smells of you,' she said childishly, barely aware of what she was saying as the brandy and mental exhaustion took their toll. Above her she thought she heard Chase make a sound which could have been a protest, but she knew that she must already be asleep and dreaming when she heard him say huskily, 'If it's the scent of me you want there's something much better than my robe.'

Because she knew it was a dream Somer knew there was no need for her to protest as she was gently rolled on to her side and the robe removed. With a sigh of pure pleasure she went into Chase's arms as he lay down beside her, burying her face in the curve of his throat.

'Mmm...' she murmured her pleasure in a low-throated whisper as her dream gave way to deeper sleep. If she couldn't actually be in Chase's arms, dreaming she was was the very next best thing.

CHAPTER TEN

SHE woke up slowly, knowing that something was different, but not knowing what, until she had surfaced enough to recognise that the pleasurable weight across her body was Chase's outflung arm, the palm of one hand possessively cupping her breast, lean brown fingers curling round the soft fullness of her body.

'Chase?'

Somer wasn't sure why she whispered his name, instead of moving away from him. Certain shaming memories were surfacing and her skin went hot and cold as she remembered how she had behaved. The disputed robe lay on the floor beyond the bed, and she cringed to remember how she had clung to it, and worse still, telling Chase why.

'Umm...'

He wasn't asleep! On the contrary, he was studying her with a lazy appreciation that suddenly made Somer realise that the bedclothes had slipped and that the creamy fullness of her breasts was clearly revealed for his leisurely inspection. And he wasn't merely looking; his thumb was rhythmically stroking across her nipple, increasing the flow of sensual sweetness pouring through her veins. Instead of repudiating him and listening to all the warnings flashing with almost incoherent urgency through her brain, she was arching delicately; stretching her body with sensual pleasure, yes, almost enjoying the predatory male glitter that darkened his eyes as they swept across her face and down over the twin curves of her breasts.

'What would you say if I told you that I needed the taste of you even more than you needed the scent of me last night?' Chase demanded with ragged urgency.

His hands pushed aside the bedclothes as he pulled her into his arms, parting her lips to taste the warmth of her mouth. There was no time for her to gather her defences. The heady pleasure of his mouth on hers had already shattered them. His chest crushed her breasts, his hands sliding down her body to mould her against him while she yielded to the urgent invasion of his tongue.

'Somer, Somer, I don't know why you're doing this, but I know what it's doing to me,' he groaned against her mouth. Her body seemed to ignite at the contact with his, nerve endings quivering into response, her body arching eagerly against him, inciting the response he couldn't suppress.

Cupping her face in his hands, Chase teased her lips. 'Open your eyes,' he commanded. 'I want to see you.'

Unwillingly Somer did so. His own were vivid blazing green, forcing her gaze along their entwined bodies, making her witness the tender caresses of his hands against her skin. Almost without his having to touch them her breasts burgeoned into urgent life, Chase tormenting them both with the chain of tiny kisses he traced downwards over her throat and down, circling round the tender crowning aureole of flesh, gradually decreasing the circles, until his own breathing became as ragged as Somer's and his tongue moved hotly against her nipple.

There was something almost dreamlike about their lovemaking, a true giving and taking that left Somer free to show him the pleasure he was giving her and to return it with hungrily aroused kisses and soft little noises of delight, her tongue stroking experimentally over the angles and planes of male flesh, testing it and finding it equally responsive to her own.

'Somer...' Chase growled warningly when she had teased him to the point where their mutual need for fulfilment was almost a physical pain for them both.

In response she wrapped her arms round him, arching her body invitingly against him, and sighing softly with pleasure when he was unable to resist her unspoken invitation.

They had never made love like this before, with an almost languorous lack of haste, that only now, with the fierce heat of Chase's body spreading through her, became an urgency that Somer responded to with shivering waves of ecstasy, that built up to a shattering climax.

'Now I know how Superman feels,' Somer murmured light-heartedly in the dizzy aftermath.

'If that's supposed to be a compliment, I've told you once I don't like substituting for anyone,' Chase drawled threateningly. His voice sounded uneven and his heart pounded against her like a sledgehammer. Somer was still feeling far enough removed from reality to say dreamily, 'No... I mean the flying...' before she fell asleep with the rumble of Chase's deep laughter still reverberating through her body.

When she woke up she was alone. She glanced at her watch and couldn't believe it. Lunch time!

She showered quickly and then went downstairs. Where was Chase?

In the dining-room she found a note. 'Had to go to the studio,' it read, 'but tonight, we're going out celebrating.' There was no indication about what they were celebrating and Somer felt small tremors of pleasure running across her skin as she remembered their early morning lovemaking. Had Chase guessed how she felt about him? Somehow that prospect didn't seem as terrifying as it once had. She even found herself humming as she walked into the kitchen to make herself a cup of coffee.

She was just finishing it when the doorbell rang. Getting up to answer it Somer was surprised to see Clancy Williams standing there. For a few, heady hours she had completely forgotten about the other woman's existence. A foolish mistake, she acknowledged painfully, as she stood back to let her walk in.

'I was driving past so I thought I'd call and tell you that Chase will be home late tonight—that's if he comes home at all,' she added maliciously. 'He's taking me out to dinner.'

'Yes, he did telephone to say that he might be delayed a little tonight,' Somer lied. Inside she wanted to weep. All the bright promise of the morning had suddenly been destroyed.

'If I hadn't gone to the States he would never have married you,' Clancy told Somer positively. 'He loves me.'

'But you did, and he did,' Somer pointed out coldly, 'and now I would like you to leave.'

When her uninvited guest had gone Somer sank back down into her chair. It had been no mere 'chance' visit. Clancy had come round deliberately to let her know that Chase would be with her this evening—and tonight, if she had her way. The phone rang making her jump.

'Somer?'

She went cold at the sound of Chase's voice. 'I'm afraid we're going to have to cancel this evening…'

Somer longed to shriek and rave at him, to tell him she knew exactly why he was cancelling their dinner date, but instead she just said calmly, 'Oh, that's all right. In fact I think I'll go down to Barnwell. I had a phone call this morning to say the decorator's keen to start. I want to show him exactly what I want done.'

'When will you be back?' Chase's voice was edged with impatience.

'Oh, I'm not sure,' Somer was deliberately vague. 'It could be several days.'

'Somer...' In the distance Somer heard another telephone ring and Chase curse. 'Look, I've got to go, I'm right in the middle of some very difficult negotiations, that's why I'm having to postpone tonight.'

'Don't worry about it,' Somer assured him coldly, 'I understand completely.'

How dare he lie to her, pretending that it was work that kept him out late in the evenings, when in reality...How dare he make love to her with tenderness and something that came perilously close to real emotion when she was just a substitute for Clancy Williams?

Having said she was going to Barnwell, she might as well do so, Somer reflected. It was true that the decorator was ready to start work and working might help to keep her mind off Chase.

For two full days it seemed as though her self-imposed solitary regime was beginning to work, and then on the third day Helena arrived. 'Chase asked me to check that you were still here,' she told Somer. 'He's been ringing without getting any response.'

Because she had been ignoring the telephone! Somer gritted her teeth.

'And why didn't you let me know you were coming down, you could have stayed with us, instead of living here on your own? It's such a large house, I wouldn't care to stay here alone at night.'

'I've been so tired that I've fallen asleep the moment my head's touched the pillow,' Somer lied. Not for the world was she going to admit to Chase's sister that she couldn't sleep without imagining that Chase was beside her; that she was in his arms.

'Any more news about your father?' Helena questioned.

'I managed to speak to him before I left London. He's safe in Saudi Arabia, and there's every chance now that the uprising will be quelled. Chase was marvellous,' she admitted unwillingly, 'if it hadn't been for him...'

'Umm. I know what you mean. He can be a real tower of strength although he does have his more vulnerable moments. He was devastated when our uncle died, even though we'd been expecting it for months. He and the old boy were really close, which is why he left everything to Chase. Of course he'd already handed over the bulk of his financial affairs and assets to Chase several years ago, and untangling them caused him more than one headache. It was then that he decided to stop working as a photographer, but he didn't want to just sit back and live off Uncle Charles's money, so he invested his own in Television West and took over his present job.

'When he first inherited I used to tease him that he was going to be another Uncle Charles and that he'd have to leave the lot to my crew because he'd never have any children of his own. I'm afraid I was being guilty of a little sisterly prying. I'd seen your photographs you see and I knew you were someone special. Chase has never gone in for that particular style of thing,' she grimaced lightly. 'At first I admit I was surprised but my dear brother can be as close as a clam when he wants to be. I even wondered at first if you were some sort of gold-digger and that you'd refused to marry him until you learned about his inheritance, but as soon as we met...'

'I didn't know anything about his inheritance,' Somer said quite truthfully.

'No, well he doesn't put it abroad. Uncle Charles was extremely wealthy, and even though he made over a large proportion of his fortune to Chase many years ago, to avoid death duties, there was still a sizeable amount to come to him when Uncle Charles died. Just as well if everything I hear about the plans you've got for this place are true,' Helena chuckled. 'How's it going?'

'Quite well.' Somer was proud of her calm tone. Inwardly she was almost dizzy with the hectic pace of her thoughts. Chase had told her that he had to marry to gain his inheritance, but unless that was something Helena didn't know, it would seem that he had lied to her. But why? Why blackmail her into marriage?

'I suppose you're anxious to rush it through so that you and Chase can move in. He's told me that he intends to take a more back-seat role in Television West. I can't say that I'm not pleased. It will be lovely having you down here, especially if you provide me with some nieces,' she added with a predatory look. 'You can tell me to mind my own business if you like, but there's a certain something about you...'

On the point of opening her mouth to strenuously deny Helena's comment, Somer paused, and then closed it again.

'Made you think, haven't I?' Helena chuckled. 'I can't wait to see my brother's face when you tell him about that.'

Only she wouldn't be telling Chase anything, Somer thought miserably, especially not the fact that it was possible that she could have conceived his child. Possible, but very far from certain, Somer reminded herself.

The plumber arrived during the afternoon, and she was too busy going over his plans with him to give detailed thought to her conversation with Helena.

Chase was the only one who could tell her if he had lied and why, but in her present vulnerable state she couldn't see herself tackling him.

She went to bed early, shivering a little as she admitted that Helena was right. The house did seem very empty at night, her small single bed distinctly lonely and uncomfortable. She slept lightly, woken several times by the church clock, finally falling into a deeper sleep in the early hours of the morning.

She didn't know what woke her. One moment she was deeply asleep, the next she was alertly awake, the tiny hairs on her arms prickling warningly. There was no sound at all from the encircling darkness, but some sixth sense warned her that she wasn't alone in the house. She thought desperately about the telephone, far too far away downstairs. A sob of pure terror rose up in her throat, and she shrank back against the bedclothes, knowing she had not simply been imagining things when she heard soft but definite footsteps on the stairs. They paused outside her door, and Somer froze.

The door was pushed open, creaking faintly in the time-honoured tradition of ghoulish movies.

'Somer, are you in there?'

'Chase!'

A horrible weak feeling invaded her senses and she felt them slip swiftly away from her. The darkness of the room became inky black and stifling. Dimly she was aware of Chase, calling her name with sharp anxiety and coming towards her.

'BETTER NOW.'

Somer opened her eyes slowly, conscious of a slow thudding behind her. Gradually she realised that the thudding was Chase's heartbeat and that she was cradled in his arms, supported against his chest.

'I fainted.' She said it almost incredulously.

'You certainly did. Hardly the most flattering welcome I've ever had.'

'But what are you doing here?'

'We had a date—remember, or didn't you get my note.'

'Your note, and your message,' Somer told him stiffly, trying to pull away. 'What happened? Did she tell you that she didn't want to share you? Is that why you're here to tell me that the charade is over?'

'She?'

'Don't pretend you don't know who I mean,' Somer said hotly. 'Clancy Williams, she called to see me several days ago—to tell me that you were taking her out to dinner, and not to expect you home until late—if at all.'

Above her head Somer heard Chase mutter something unflattering. 'And you believed her? After what had happened that morning?'

Somer tried to sound nonchalant. 'So you made love to me…so…I'm hardly the first…'

'And of course I'm not Hollister. Even though your body responds to mine as though it had been designed for it,' Chase said bitterly. 'Somer, I didn't drive down here in the middle of the night to argue with you.'

'Then what did you come for?'

'This.'

She was already in his arms, and there was no way she could avoid the fierce possession of his kiss. She tried to resist but it was impossible. Her own hunger joined Chase in the battle against her.

'If it was kisses you wanted,' she forced herself to say shakily when Chase released her, 'I'm surprised you didn't go to Clancy.'

'She doesn't stock the right brand.' It was dark, but she could readily imagine the lazy, seductive smile curving Chase's mouth. 'And I'm very fussy about my kisses. You see I developed a taste for these particularly rare ones a long time ago.'

'Chase, stop it,' Somer protested huskily. 'You keep on playing games and I can't keep pace with them.'

'Games?' She felt his body tense. 'Such as?'

'Such as telling me that you had to marry to inherit your uncle's money.'

'Ah, my dear sister's been talking, has she?'

'So you did lie to me…but why? Why try to blackmail me…all that trouble you went to…why, Chase?'

'Why? You mean to say you really don't know?' He laughed harshly. 'Somer, have you any idea what you did to me five years ago? God, you were like a kick in the gut. I reacted to you the way I'd never reacted to any woman. I wanted you and you seemed to want me too. I knew you were young…too young…. I saw you in the lift and spent the rest of that day arguing against trying to see you again, and then you came up to me and virtually invited yourself out with me…and then what happened?

'I came down to earth with a bump. I knew what you wanted from me, or so I thought and you weren't the first. Any good photographer soon gets to learn that there'll always be those women who are ready to make themselves available in return for first-class shots of themselves. When you asked me to photograph you I wanted to strangle you, even though part of me had been waiting for you to ask. You were too young and too promiscuous, or so I thought until you knocked the ground from under me by telling me the truth.

'I could have killed you, do you realise that? You didn't want *me* at all, you told me naïvely, you just wanted a man, any man to take your virginity, and God help me, you'd picked on me. You'll never know how tempted I was…how much I wanted to take you there and then and stamp you as my possession, to make love to you until you couldn't think straight and then…'

'Then discard me as punishment,' Somer put in huskily, 'instead unwittingly, you conceived an even better punishment. You made me doubt my own sexuality. Andrew had rejected me and now you were rejecting me.'

'And mine was the rejection you remembered?'

Somer didn't deny it.

'It wasn't like you think at all, Somer,' Chase told her softly. 'After you ran out on me like that I tried to find you. I realised you were upset and I wanted to see you, to explain to you why I had to stop, why I couldn't make love to you.'

'And *why* couldn't you?' Somer asked painfully. 'Initially you seemed to want me.'

'Oh, I wanted you all right. I more than wanted you, that was the whole trouble. I didn't want to hurt my pride that that was all you wanted from me. But when I tried to find out who you were and where you'd gone I drew a complete blank. Judith was on reception when I made enquiries about you and she pretended not to remember you. She even searched through the visitors' book to find your name and address, but she told me you mustn't have signed in.'

'Why?' Somer was amazed. 'Why should she do that?'

'Who knows? Perhaps because she sensed even then that Hollister wasn't totally immune to you, no matter what he might have said.

'When I got back home I developed your photographs. I wanted to burn them, to destroy all my memories of you completely, but every time I tried to do it I couldn't. Helena found one of them. It was in my wallet...'

'You carried a photograph of me in your wallet?'

'Right next to my heart,' Chase told her with wry self-mockery. 'I reckoned that was the closest I'd ever get to you. I used to think about you and torture myself wondering who you'd eventually given yourself to, and whether he'd felt the same way about you as I did.'

'And how was that?' How calm she sounded, and yet her heart was beating out a wild tattoo of hope.

'What the hell do you think?' Chase challenged, drawing away from her and standing up. He walked across the window and remained silhouetted there, a barely definable tension hardening the muscles of his body. 'I wasn't a boy, even then, Somer, unsure of my feelings, or ignorant in any way about the depth or intensity of them. I know it sounds trite to say this, but I fell in love with you almost on sight. Oh, I fought against it, I told myself you were just another pretty, promiscuous kid on the make and that I'd play you along, get you out of my system, and no harm done on either side. But I knew the harm had already been done when you asked me to photograph you, and then when you told me the truth! Now do you understand why I couldn't make love to you then?' he grated thickly. 'And why I couldn't resist the temptation to do exactly that when you told me why there'd been no one else?

'The first time I made love to you was in anger—I thought you'd been with Hollister; I couldn't believe it when I discovered you were still a virgin. You told me it was because you were still in love with him. Was that true, Somer?'

It was like preparing to leap blindfolded into space, terrifying, exhilarating, requiring an act of courage and faith, and it took all her strength to do it.

'No,' she admitted softly. 'No, Chase, I lied to you.'

'Because…' he pressed softly.

'Because I loved you,' Somer murmured, 'even though I didn't want to admit it to myself. I knew the first time you touched me after our marriage, that I wasn't incapable of feeling, and I knew exactly why I hadn't been able to respond to anyone else. I told myself that you were to blame, that you had destroyed my ability to respond because you had rejected me, but it wasn't entirely true. If you had made love to me when we first met the result would have been exactly the same.'

'Oh no, it would not,' Chase corrected explosively, turning round and striding determinedly towards her. 'If I had made love to you then we'd have been married long before now…I wouldn't have needed to blackmail you. I couldn't believe it when I saw your photograph in the papers. Once I knew properly who you were I found out as much as I could about you, then I laid my plans. I worked out everything in advance, including the phoney will. I wanted you so badly that this time I wasn't going to let anything stand in the way.'

'Not even Clancy Williams?' Somer said provocatively. 'And you can pretend there wasn't anything between you? I saw how much she wanted you.'

'Yes, you did, didn't you?' Chase agreed wryly. 'All part of my nefarious master plan—a plan which backfired dismally. I wanted you to be as jealous of me as I was of you! I always knew exactly what Clancy was—she'd made a couple of plays for me in the past. Half the reason she wants me now is that I've become unavailable, and she can't bear frustration—any more than I can,' he added significantly. 'I knew you responded to me sexually, you see, and I thought that if I could just make you jealous, it might be like a proverbial spark to dry tinder…that in the wake of jealousy would come love.'

'Umm…only you'd got them the wrong way round. The love was already there.'

'And you don't love Hollister?'

'No. I don't believe I ever did, but I was terrified you would guess how I felt, so I let you believe I loved him. That time when you saw us together, I hadn't known he was in London.'

'Will you forgive me for blackmailing you into marriage, and forcing you to share my bed…or rather my sister's bed?'

'I'll forgive you that—I think,' Somer agreed. 'But I'm not sure if I'm going to be able to forgive you all those nights I slept alone.'

'It was the only way I could keep my hands off you,' Chase admitted, groaning softly. 'I've been up to my neck in negotiations for the American rights of Clancy's new series, and it's been like fighting my way through a quagmire. She's been as difficult as all hell, and I haven't been able to tell her to get lost until the series was all tied up. Sleeping with you at Helena's was absolute purgatory… I told myself that separation was the only thing that was going to stop me from going raving mad. But those few nights…waking up with you in my arms was sheer bloody hell. The only thing that stopped you from being well and truly ravished was the thought of those brats of hers bursting in on us. I still have nightmares about it happening and Ben airing his knowledge about the human reproductive system over the breakfast table.'

Somer giggled.

'It's all very well for you,' Chase told her lazily. 'Are you really sure you love me?' He said the words lightly, but Somer could feel the fine tremor in his fingers as they touched her face, finding her mouth and then stroking along her throat.

'Shall I tell you…or show you?' she murmured softly. Her lips seemed to find his jawline without any hesitation and she just caught his softly suppressed groan as she teased tender kisses over his unshaven skin.

'Both,' Chase pleaded hoarsely. 'I've been so starved for you, Somer, that I need all the reassurance you can give me. Contrary to what you might think, I'm not in the habit of blackmailing people, or of forcing them into unwanted marriages. There were times when I woke up thinking I had gone stark raving mad.'

'And now?' Somer asked, still busily engaged on the delirious discovery that Chase's skin was every bit as responsive to her kisses as hers was to his.

'Now, modest always to a fault, I am forced to concede that I was gifted with a brilliant foresight, permitted to very few men. And you still haven't told me that you love me,' he reminded her softly, pulling her into his arms and lowering her against the mattress.

Momentarily Somer sobered. 'I love you, Chase, in all the ways there are. The night you traced my father for me I wanted badly to tell you then…'

'And I thought I *had* told you just how much you mean to me,' Chase whispered. 'I was going to come home that night and admit what I had done, I couldn't wait any longer… I wanted you at my side as my wife…not someone I had forced into an unwanted relationship. I told myself there was something there…that we could make it work.'

'When you rang up I thought you were having second thoughts…that you were spending the evening with Clancy. I wanted to dismember you.'

'Very blood-thirsty. I was having dinner with her, and

her agent…and the American series producers, and half a dozen other people so that we could thrash out the final details. The series will bump our ratings sky-high, and I can tell you I heaved a mammoth sigh of relief when she finally signed. Clancy's problem is that she's so used to playing a *femme fatale* that she can't believe that in real life she's more than resistible. At least as far as I'm concerned.'

'Fire-proof, are you?' Somer teased.

'Not where you're concerned. Want to put it to the test?' His lips were brushing the tender skin beneath her ear, and Somer gave herself up to the heady pleasure of enjoying the shivery sensations spreading through her skin.

'This time we've got all the time in the world,' Chase told her huskily, 'and no insecurities.'

'So why is it that I get the feeling that you're a man in a very big hurry?' Somer teased breathlessly only seconds later, when she knew without a trace of shame that her body was already craving his immediate possession.

'*I'm* in a hurry?' Chase tormented back. 'So it's all one-sided, is it?'

LATER THEY made love again, Chase groaning that he would be glad when they could share a decent-sized bed. 'You know what the trouble with you is,' Somer teased. 'You've no sense of adventure.'

'Oh, is that what it is?'

Warm male laughter filled her ears. 'Well, we'll see who's got a sense of adventure.' With breathtaking skill he touched and caressed her with an intimacy that left her shaken with the knowledge of her own responses, and as though he knew how she felt Chase enfolded her in his arms, murmuring soft words of love against her skin.

When she woke up in the morning, Somer glanced at him to discover that he was still asleep.

He woke up almost immediately and smiled at her.

'Still love me?'

'More than ever,' Somer assured him, 'and I'll love you twice as much if...'

She had been about to say, if you go and make me a cup of tea, but the very act of lifting her head from the pillow provoked a wave of nausea that had Chase following her abrupt flight to the bathroom.

'Somer...what's wrong, are you all right?'

He looked anxious, almost grey, as he surveyed her pale face. 'You, an uncle four times over, and you still don't recognise the morning sickness when you see it?' Somer scoffed, when she had recovered, watching the enlightenment drawn on his face. 'Helena would be ashamed of you.'

'A child...you're carrying my child.' He came across to her, and gathered her in his arms, his hand spread possessively across her still flat stomach.

'*Child?*' Somer's eyebrows rose. 'Do you think so? *I* was thinking we ought to insure against twins.'

An hour later as they sat in the chaos of the kitchen drinking coffee Chase said quietly, 'Are you really happy about all this, Somer? A husband...a family? Six months ago.'

'Six months ago all I had in my life was my father and a computer,' Somer told him briskly. 'My father I want to keep, but the computer—I'll gladly trade it for other things. Chase, I love you.' She stood up, slipping her arms round him, feeling his body take heat from the contact with hers.

'Umm,' Chase whispered huskily. 'Do you think what-

ever you've got in there will object if I take you back to
bed and make love to you again?'

'It might not, and I certainly wouldn't, but Helena is
heading for the back door and I'm pretty sure she would.'

Chase released her with a groan just as his sister stepped
into the room.

'Chase!' She looked surprised to see him. 'You never
said Chase was coming down,' she said to Somer.

'She didn't know,' Chase grinned at his sister. 'I suddenly decided I couldn't do without her any longer, and
now I'm taking her back to London with me. She needs
someone to take care of her. She's been doing far too
much.'

'Far too much of something,' Helena agreed drily, adding, with a knowing grin, 'am I right in thinking this "taking care of her" involves a good deal of...'

'Never you mind what it involves,' Chase interrupted,
returning her grin, and later when she had gone Somer
mentally blessed her sister-in-law, for not giving in to the
temptation Somer had seen bursting from her to tell Chase
that she was well aware of the reasons for his excessive
high spirits.

Instead of going out to dinner to celebrate as Chase had
planned, they ate quietly at home. Somer cooked for them,
and then curled up on the settee, her head in Chase's lap,
while they talked. Soon talk gave way to languid silences
and small murmurs of pleasure.

'Love me for ever,' Chase muttered thickly, releasing
the rosy peak of her breast from lips that had caressed it
to hard desire. 'I can hardly believe it's true; that at last
you're mine.'

'WELL, Ambassador, what do you think about your granddaughters?' Somer grinned as she caught the note of pride

in Chase's voice. Their twins were three months old, and almost identical in looks if not in personality. Only this morning they had been christened and had behaved with perfect propriety as befitted the granddaughters of one of Her Majesty's Government officials. Now they grinned gummily up from the arms of their father, waving small pink bootee-clad feet, and gurgling.

Barnwell was now a real home, Somer thought with pleasure, complete with dismantled bike bits. Ben had brought the bicycle round six weeks ago to ask Chase to help him fix it, and it was still lying on the laundry-room floor.

'What's making you so pensive?' Chase murmured, coming across to her.

He had been there when the twins were born, and their birth had drawn them even closer together.

'I was just wondering how long it would take you to master bike mechanics,' she said vaguely. 'I mean, if in the future...'

Chase caught her drift almost immediately and went pale. 'You're not...?

'Not yet,' she grinned, adding shyly, 'not for any want of trying on your part I might add.'

'While you, of course, merely endured,' Chase teased back. 'I can see I'm falling down seriously on my duties. Tonight, my love, I shall endeavour to do better.'

'What are you two whispering about?' Ben asked curiously. 'You're always whispering and hugging, and kissing.... It's soppy.'

'Helena,' Chase roared, 'come and remove this obnoxious brat of yours. In fact,' he added in a low voice to Somer, 'I'd like it if she'd remove the whole damn lot of them, I want very much to be alone with my wife.' He bent his head and brushed her lips with his, his kiss a pledge of all that they had already shared and a promise of all that was to come. It was a miracle that they had ever met once, never mind twice.

'I love you, Chase Lorimer,' she whispered to him, 'but right now we have guests.'

'Later you can *show* me how much you love me, as well as telling me.'

And later she did.

Harlequin Romance®

Delightful

Affectionate

Romantic

Emotional

Tender

Original

Daring

Riveting

Enchanting

Adventurous

Moving

Harlequin Romance—the
series that has it all!

HROM-G

HARLEQUIN PRESENTS®

The world's bestselling romance series...
The series that brings you your favorite authors,
month after month:

Helen Bianchin...Emma Darcy
Lynne Graham...Penny Jordan
Miranda Lee...Sandra Morton
Anne Mather...Carole Mortimer
Susan Napier...Michelle Reid

and many more uniquely talented authors!

Wealthy, powerful, gorgeous men...
Women who have feelings just like your own...
The stories you love, set in exotic, glamorous locations...

HARLEQUIN PRESENTS,
Seduction and passion guaranteed!

Harlequin® Historical

From rugged lawmen and
valiant knights to defiant heiresses
and spirited frontierswomen,
Harlequin Historicals will
capture your imagination with
their dramatic scope, passion
and adventure.

Harlequin Historicals...
they're too good to miss!

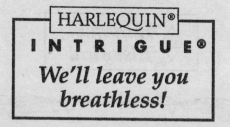

HARLEQUIN SUPERROMANCE®

...there's more to the story!

Superromance. A *big* satisfying read about unforgettable characters. Each month we offer *four* very different stories that range from family drama to adventure and mystery, from highly emotional stories to romantic comedies—and much more! Stories about people you'll believe in and care about. Stories too compelling to put down....

Our authors are among today's *best* romance writers. You'll find familiar names and talented newcomers. Many of them are award winners—and you'll see why!

If you want the biggest and best in romance fiction, you'll get it from Superromance!

Available wherever Harlequin books are sold.

HARLEQUIN®

Makes any time special.™

Upbeat, all-American romances about the pursuit of love, marriage and family.

Two brand-new, full-length romantic comedy novels for one low price.

Harlequin® Historical

Rich and vivid historical romances that capture the imagination with their dramatic scope, passion and adventure.

HARLEQUIN®
Temptation

Sexy, sassy and seductive— Temptation is hot sizzling romance.

HARLEQUIN®
SUPERROMANCE

A bigger romance read with more plot, more story-line variety, more pages and a romance that's evocatively explored.

Harlequin Romance®

Love stories that capture the essence of traditional romance.

HARLEQUIN®
INTRIGUE®

Dynamic mysteries with a thrilling combination of breathtaking romance and heart-stopping suspense.

HARLEQUIN  PRESENTS®

Meet sophisticated men of the world and captivating women in glamorous, international settings.